# PERSEUS AND MEDUSA

## A GRAPHIC NOVEL
### BY BLAKE A. HOENA & DANIEL FERRAN

STONE ARCH BOOKS
A CAPSTONE IMPRINT

Graphic Revolve is published by Stone Arch Books
A Capstone Imprint
1710 Roe Crest Drive, North Mankato, Minnesota 56003
www.capstonepub.com



Cataloging-in-Publication Data is available at the Library of Congress website.
Hardcover ISBN: 978-1-4965-0020-5
Paperback ISBN: 978-1-4965-0039-7

Summary: Young Perseus grows up, unaware of his royal birth. Before he can claim his heritage, the hero is ordered to slay a hideous monster named Medusa, whose gaze turns men into solid stone. How can the youth fight an enemy he cannot even look at?

Common Core back matter written by Dr. Katie Monnin.

Color by Eve, Sebastián Facio, and Daniel Ferran.

Designer: Bob Lentz
Assistant Designer: Peggie Carley
Editor: Donald Lemke
Assistant Editor: Sean Tulien
Creative Director: Heather Kindseth
Editorial Director: Michael Dahl
Publisher: Ashley C. Andersen Zantop

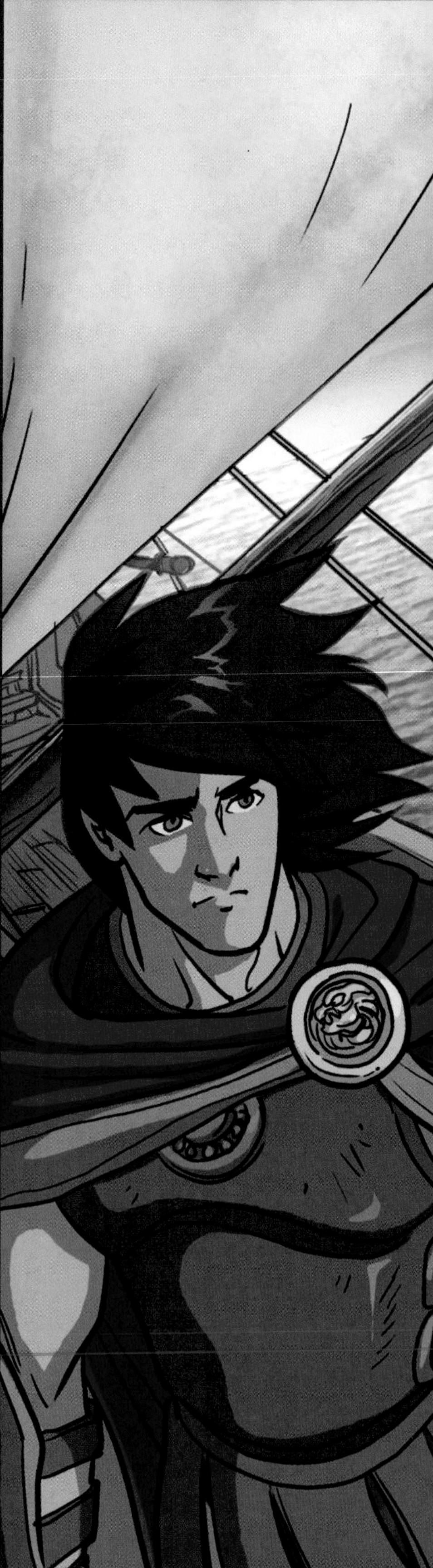

Printed in the United States 4164

# TABLE OF CONTENTS

ABOUT ANCIENT MONSTERS.................................................................... 4

CAST OF CHARACTERS........................................................................... 6

CHAPTER 1
BIRTH OF A HERO.................................................................................. 8

CHAPTER 2
AN IMPOSSIBLE QUEST........................................................................ 16

CHAPTER 3
EYE OF THE WITCHES.......................................................................... 26

CHAPTER 4
MEDUSA!............................................................................................... 36

CHAPTER 5
THE RESCUE......................................................................................... 48

CHAPTER 6
THE EVIL KING...................................................................................... 56

ABOUT THE RETELLING AUTHOR AND ILLUSTRATOR.......................... 66

GLOSSARY............................................................................................. 67

COMMON CORE ALIGNED READING AND WRITING QUESTIONS............ 68

# ABOUT ANCIENT MONSTERS

The ancient Greek myths contain legends of many strange and interesting monsters. Some of them threatened the safety of mankind, while others served important roles in preserving the safety of humans and gods alike . . .

**Briareus** was a giant with one hundred arms. He fought with his brothers and with Zeus against the Titans.

**Python** was a gigantic dragon that terrorized Greece. It was eventually defeated by the powerful arrows of **Apollo**, god of the sun.

The **Chimera** was one of the deadliest creatures of Greek myth. The monster was part dragon, part goat, and part lion. And it could breathe fire. It was finally slain by the hero **Bellerophon** who rode on the flying horse, **Pegasus**. Bellerophon attacked the monster from the air, avoiding its fiery breath.

Not all of the Greek monsters were enemies of the gods. **Cerberus** was appointed by the gods to guard the gates of the underworld, called Hades. He was a monstrous three-headed dog with the lower body of a snake, with even more serpents sprouting from his back. He made sure that only the spirits of the dead entered Hades — the living were not welcome there. More importantly, Cerberus prevented anyone from leaving the world of the dead after they had arrived, ensuring that the spirits of the dead would remain in the underworld instead of haunting the living.

Each Greek monster had its own unique and special qualities, but most had one thing in common: a mother. **Echidna**, who lived deep underground, gave birth to almost all of Greek mythology's evil creatures, including Cerberus himself! Echidna's face was beautiful and fair, but she had large wings and a serpent's body. She was so monstrous that she tried to attack the Greek gods themselves. Despite her ferocity, she was utterly defeated. However, the gods allowed Echidna and her children to live so they could test the heroes of Greece.

# CAST OF CHARACTERS

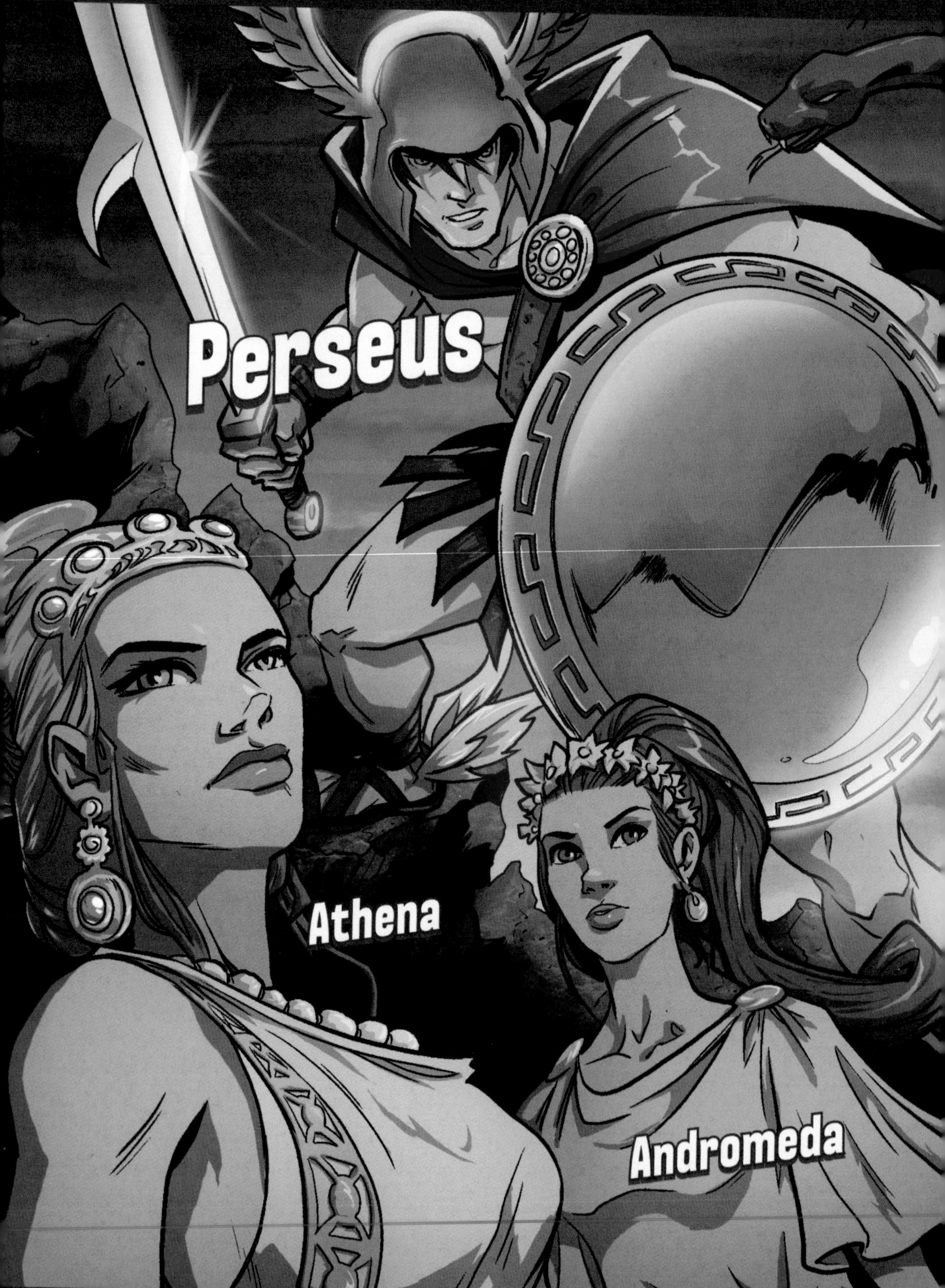
Perseus
Athena
Andromeda

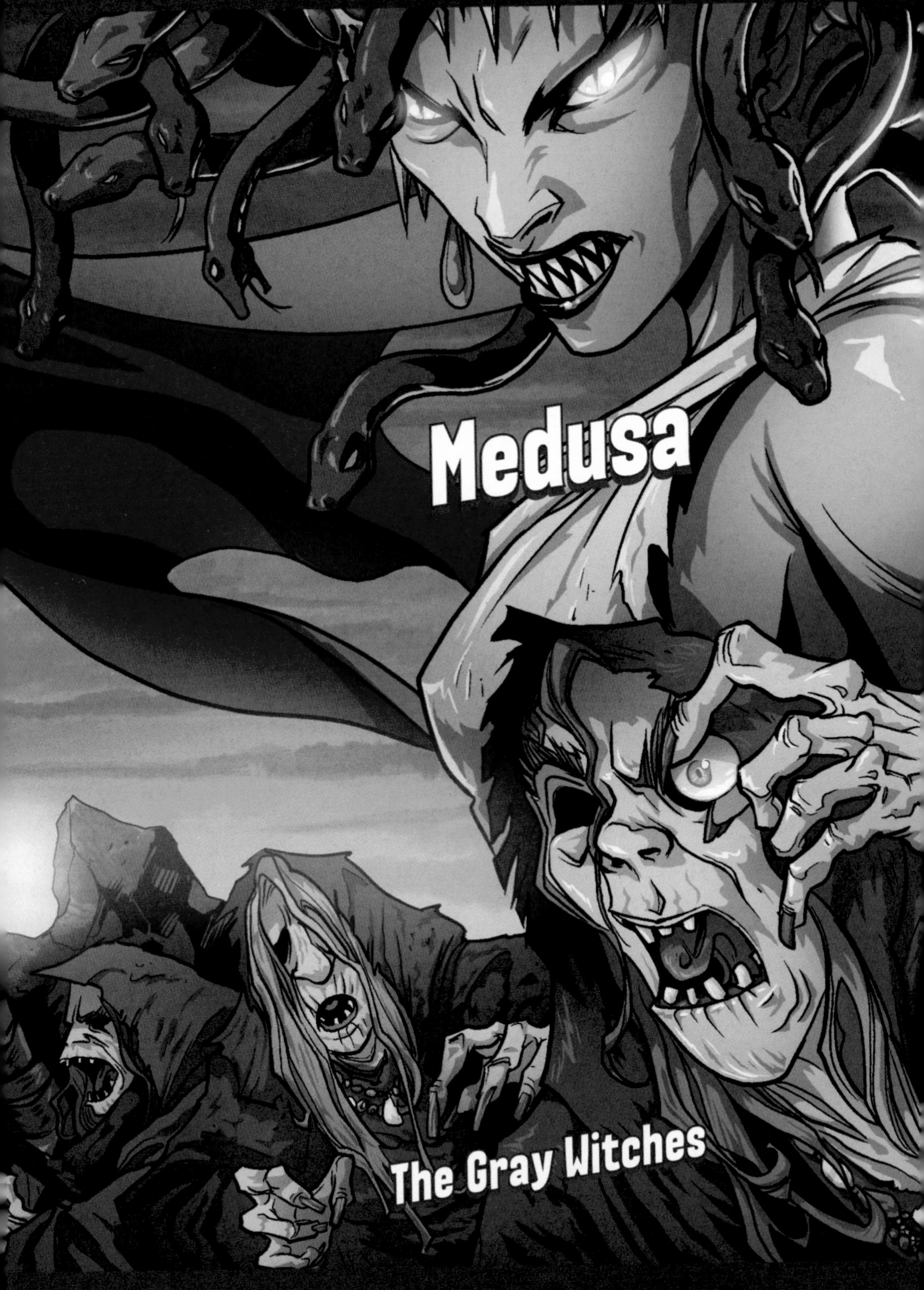
Medusa
The Gray Witches

CHAPTER 1
# BIRTH OF A HERO

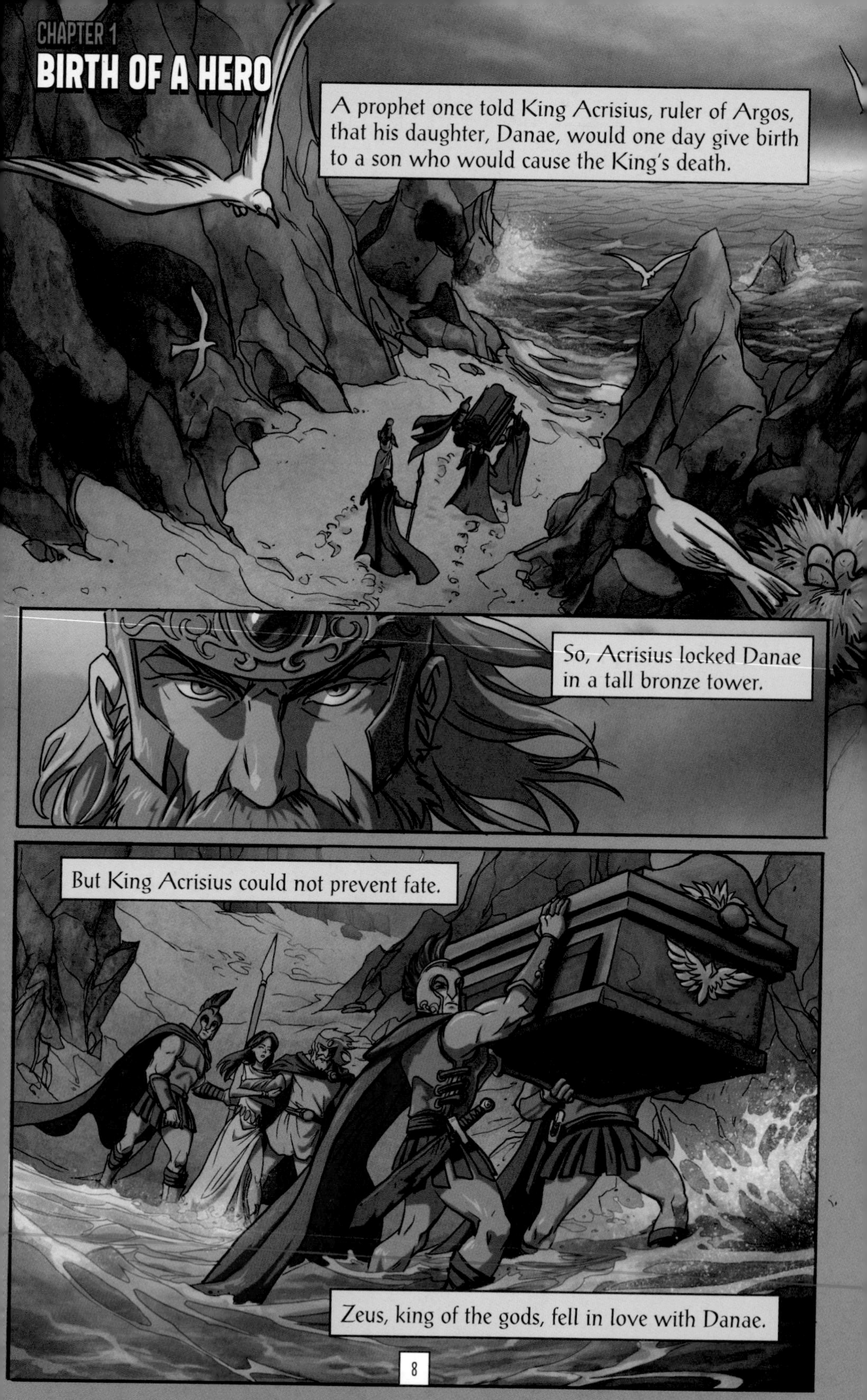
A prophet once told King Acrisius, ruler of Argos, that his daughter, Danae, would one day give birth to a son who would cause the King's death.
So, Acrisius locked Danae in a tall bronze tower.
But King Acrisius could not prevent fate.
Zeus, king of the gods, fell in love with Danae.

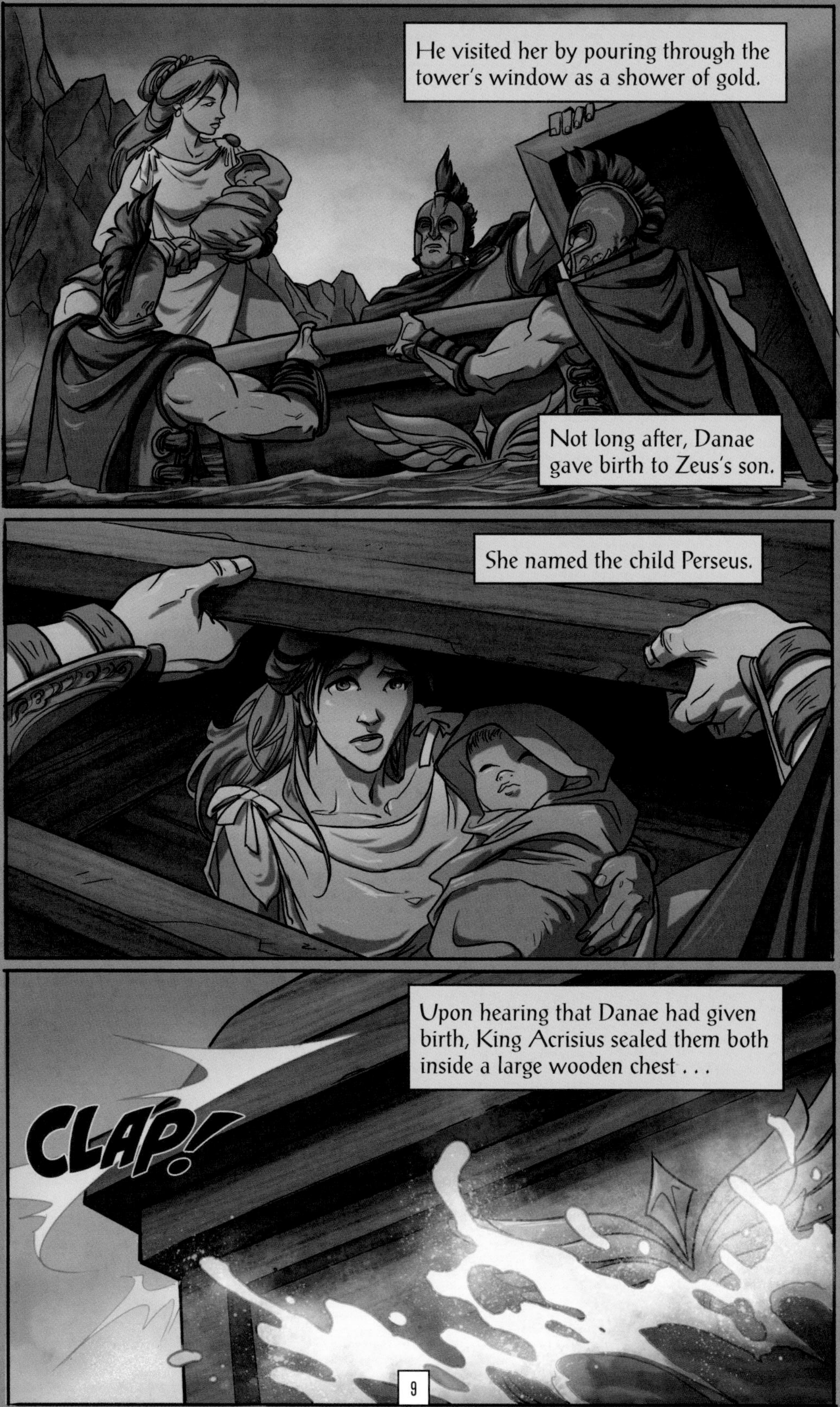
He visited her by pouring through the tower's window as a shower of gold.
Not long after, Danae gave birth to Zeus's son.
She named the child Perseus.
Upon hearing that Danae had given birth, King Acrisius sealed them both inside a large wooden chest . . .
CLAP!

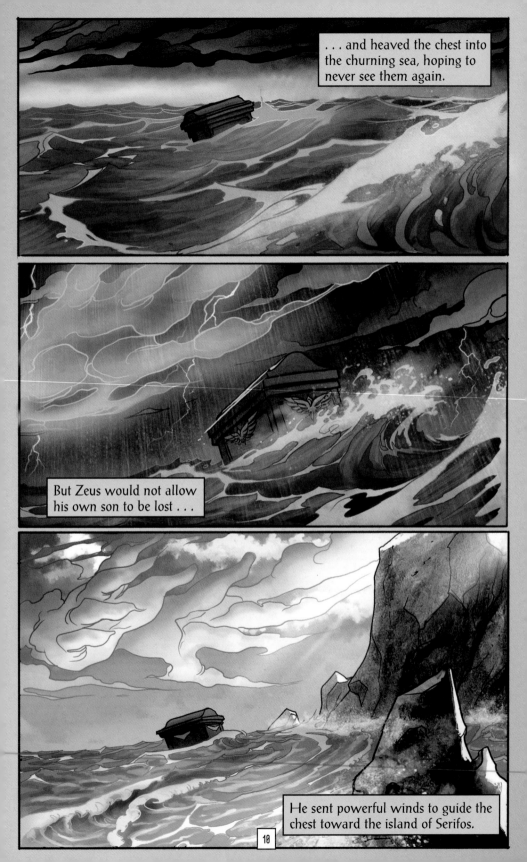

. . . and heaved the chest into the churning sea, hoping to never see them again.

But Zeus would not allow his own son to be lost . . .

He sent powerful winds to guide the chest toward the island of Serifos.

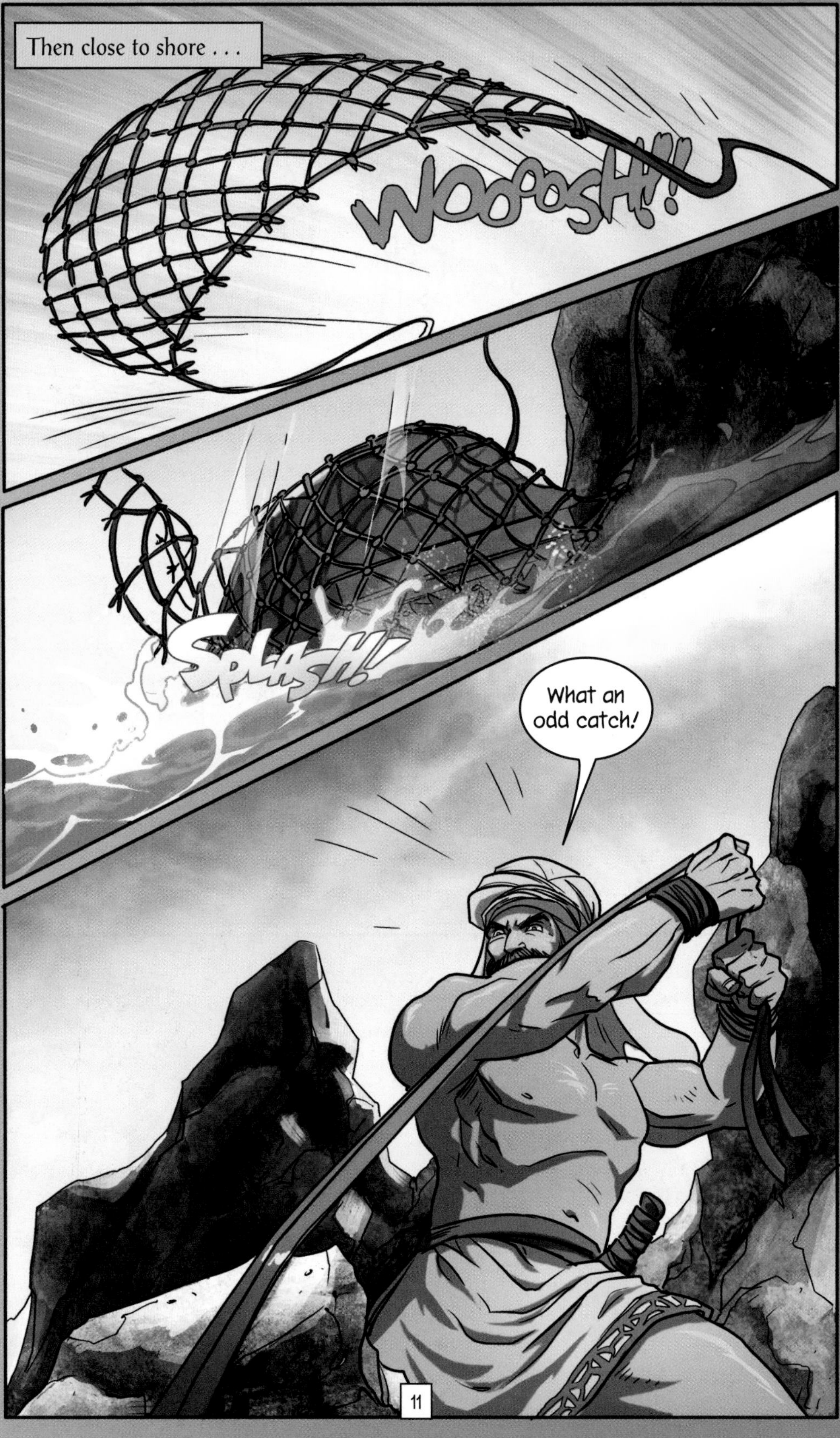
Then close to shore . . .
WOOOOSH!!
SPLASH!
What an odd catch!

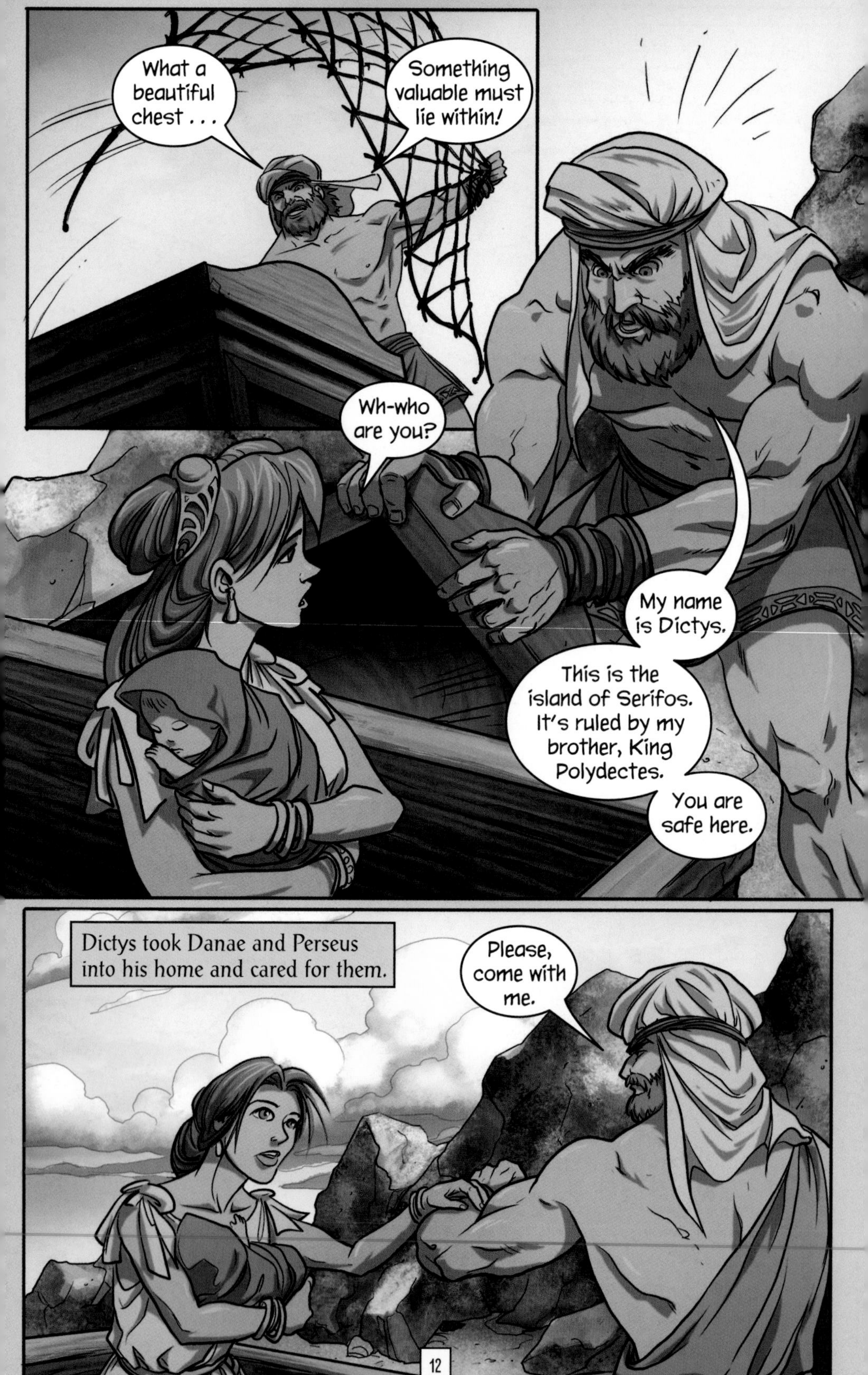
What a beautiful chest . . .
Something valuable must lie within!
Wh-who are you?
My name is Dictys.
This is the island of Serifos. It's ruled by my brother, King Polydectes.
You are safe here.
Dictys took Danae and Perseus into his home and cared for them.
Please, come with me.

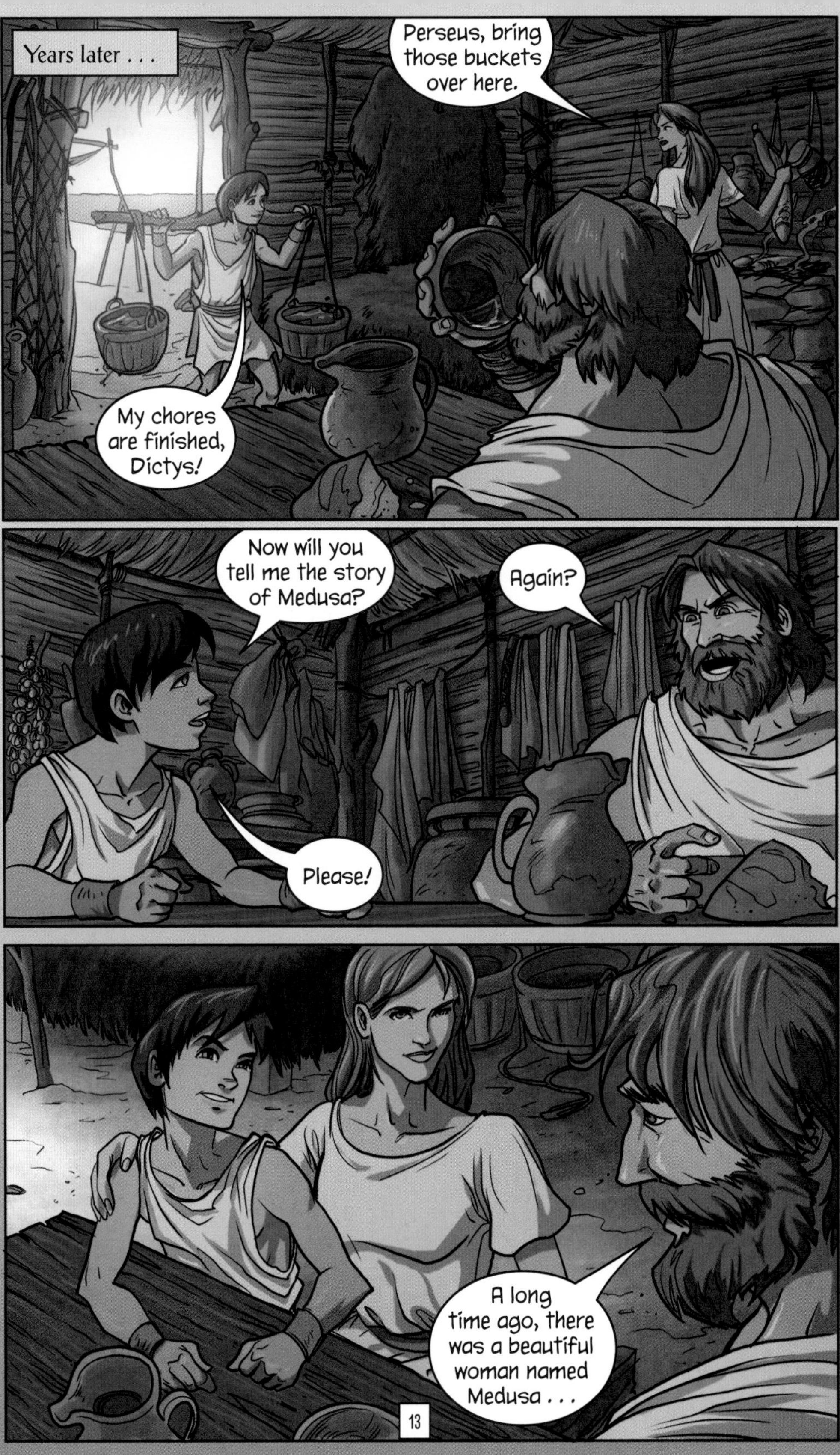
Years later . . .
Perseus, bring those buckets over here.
My chores are finished, Dictys!
Now will you tell me the story of Medusa?
Again?
Please!
A long time ago, there was a beautiful woman named Medusa . . .

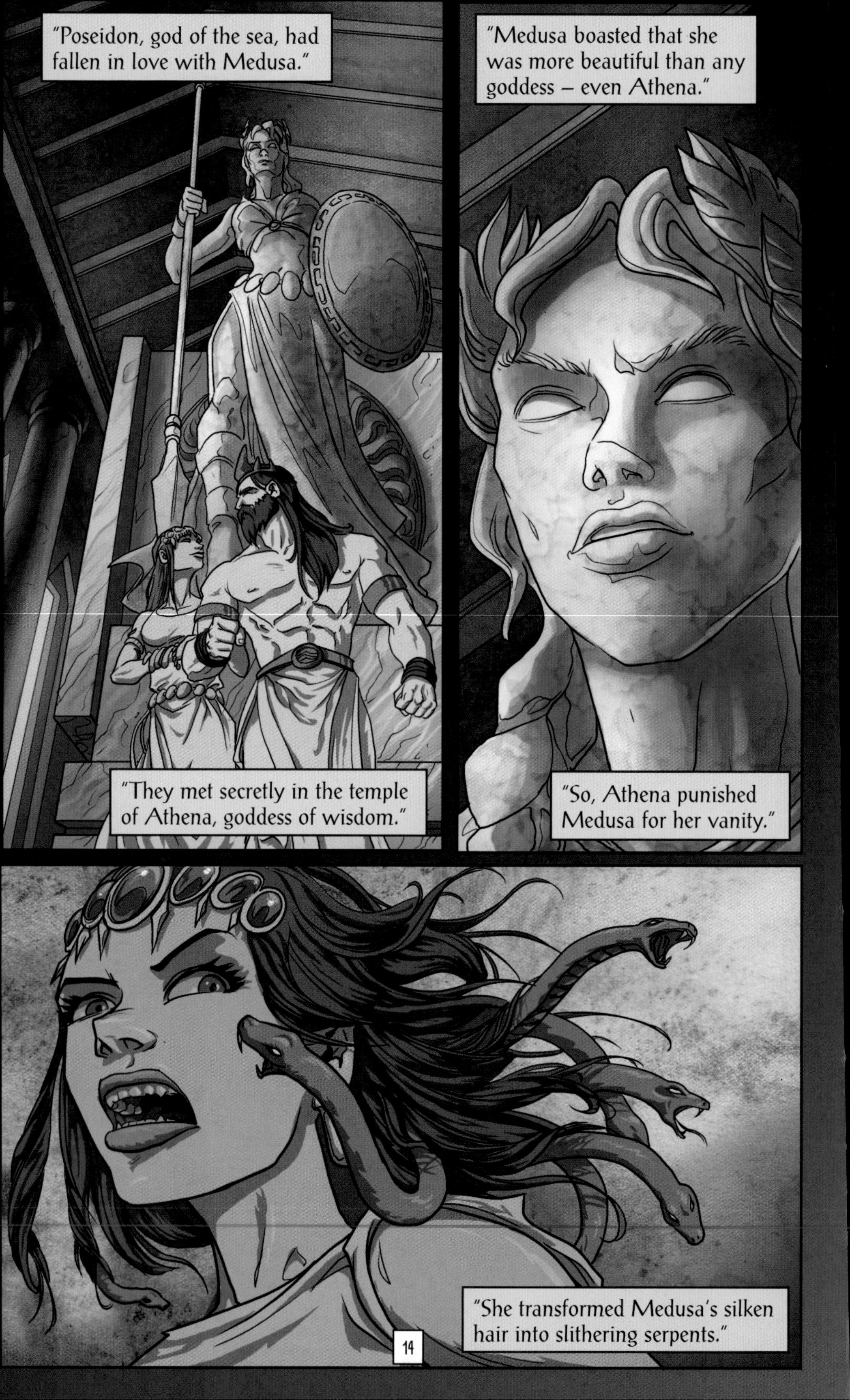
"Poseidon, god of the sea, had fallen in love with Medusa."
"They met secretly in the temple of Athena, goddess of wisdom."
"Medusa boasted that she was more beautiful than any goddess – even Athena."
"So, Athena punished Medusa for her vanity."
"She transformed Medusa's silken hair into slithering serpents."

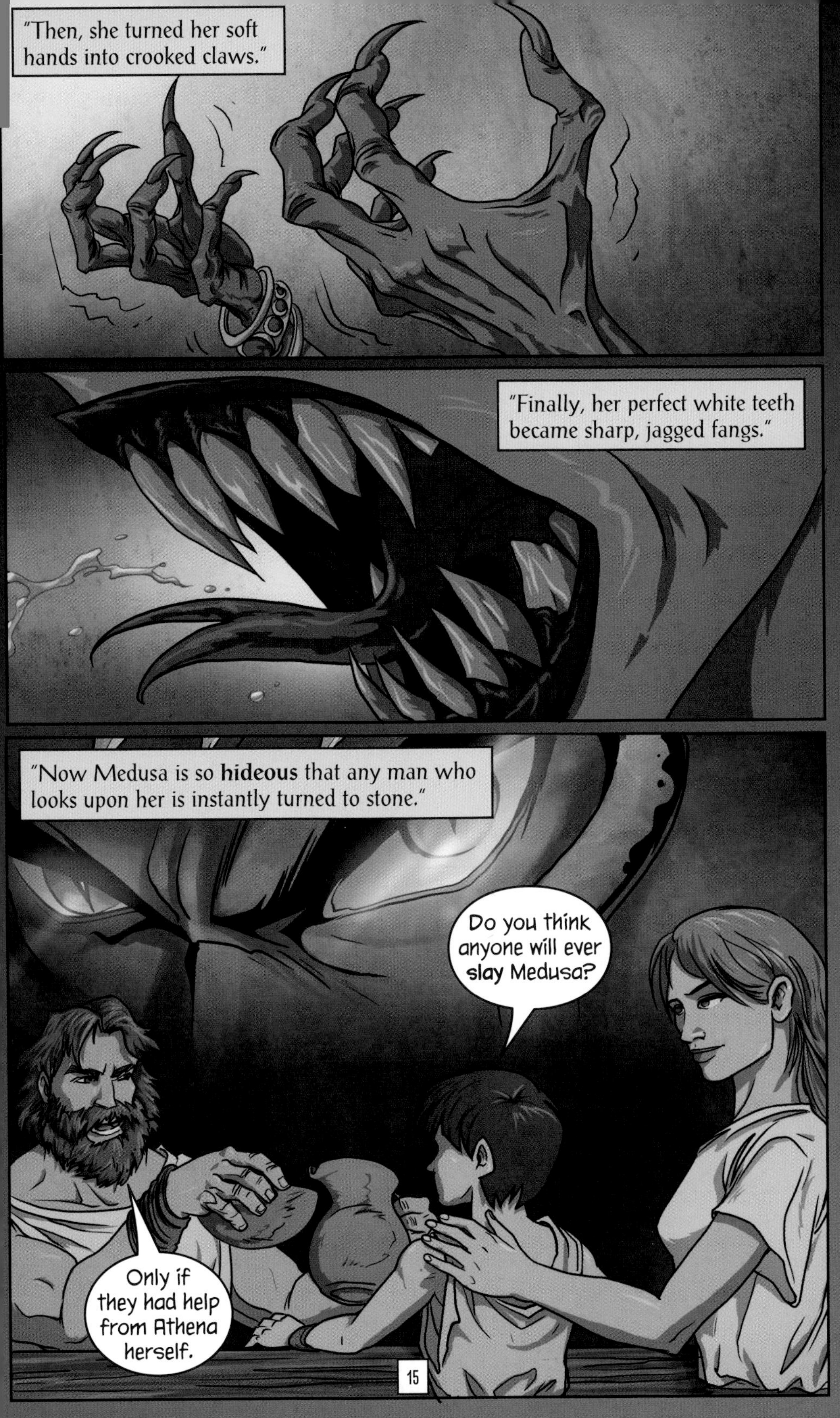
"Then, she turned her soft hands into crooked claws."
"Finally, her perfect white teeth became sharp, jagged fangs."
"Now Medusa is so **hideous** that any man who looks upon her is instantly turned to stone."
Do you think anyone will ever **slay** Medusa?
Only if they had help from Athena herself.

CHAPTER 2
# AN IMPOSSIBLE QUEST

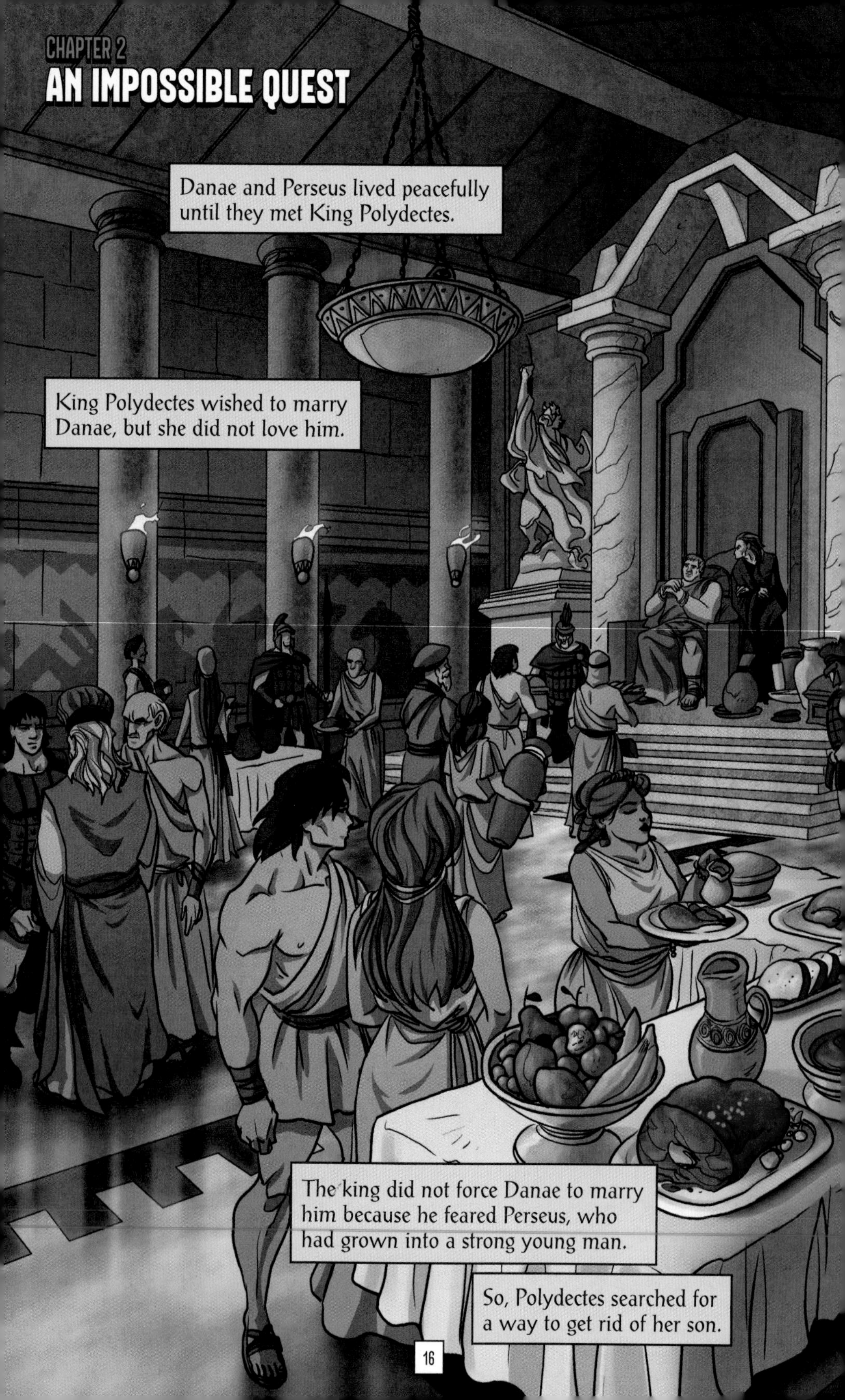
Danae and Perseus lived peacefully until they met King Polydectes.
King Polydectes wished to marry Danae, but she did not love him.
The king did not force Danae to marry him because he feared Perseus, who had grown into a strong young man.
So, Polydectes searched for a way to get rid of her son.

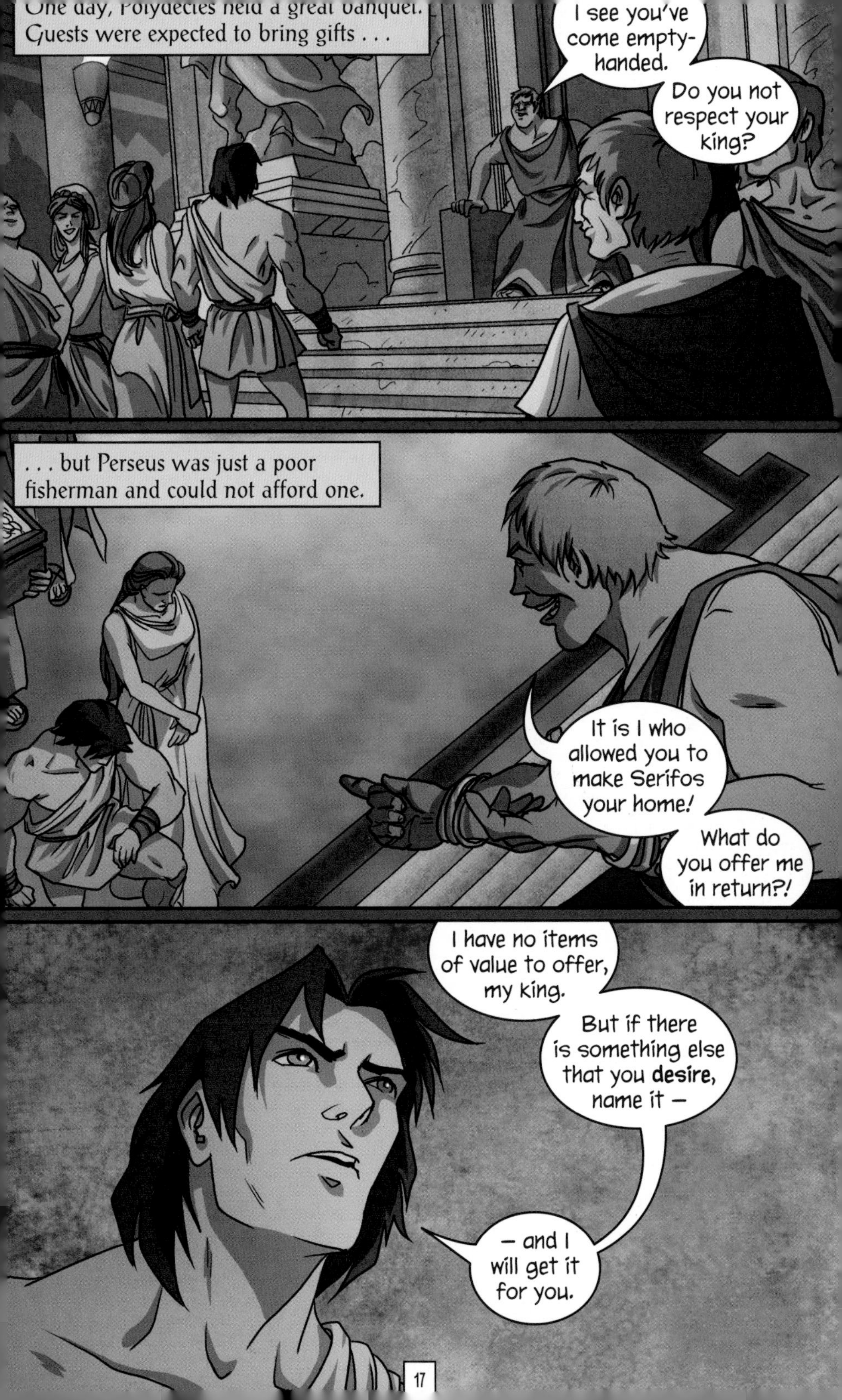
One day, Polydectes held a great banquet. Guests were expected to bring gifts . . .
I see you've come empty-handed.
Do you not respect your king?
. . . but Perseus was just a poor fisherman and could not afford one.
It is I who allowed you to make Serifos your home!
What do you offer me in return?!
I have no items of value to offer, my king.
But if there is something else that you **desire**, name it –
– and I will get it for you.

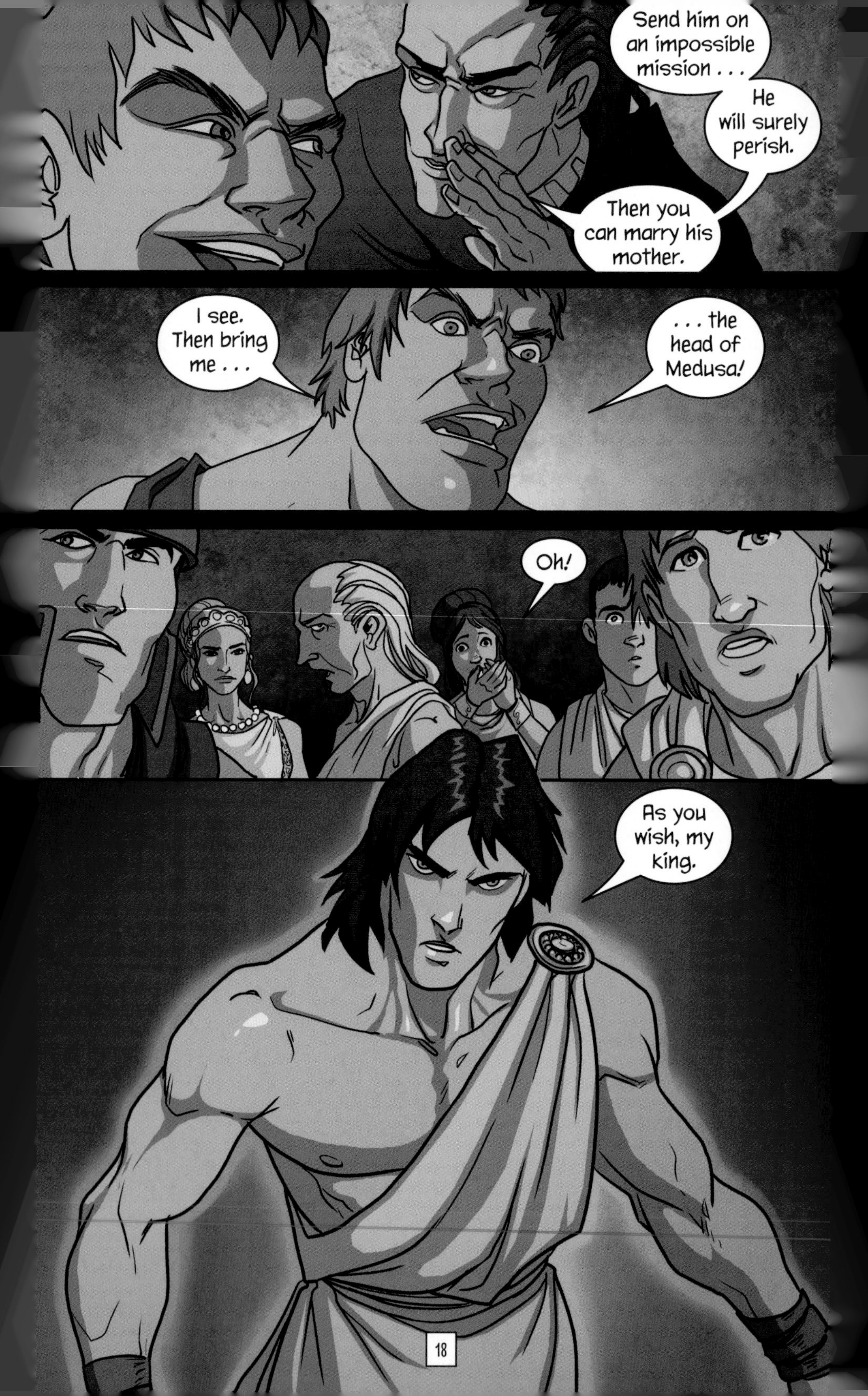
Send him on an impossible mission . . .
He will surely perish.
Then you can marry his mother.
I see. Then bring me . . .
. . . the head of Medusa!
Oh!
As you wish, my king.

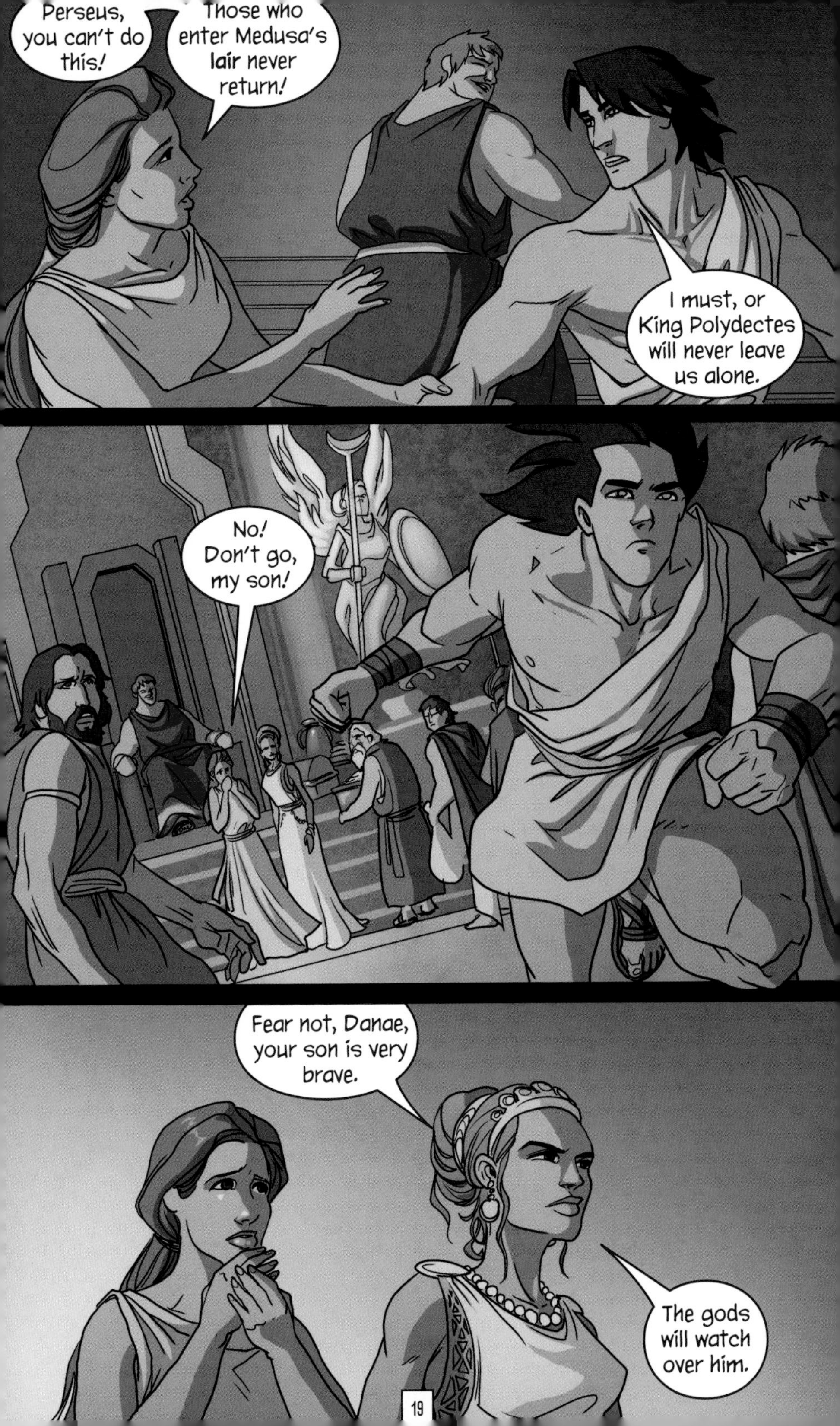
Perseus, you can't do this!
Those who enter Medusa's **lair** never return!
I must, or King Polydectes will never leave us alone.
No! Don't go, my son!
Fear not, Danae, your son is very brave.
The gods will watch over him.

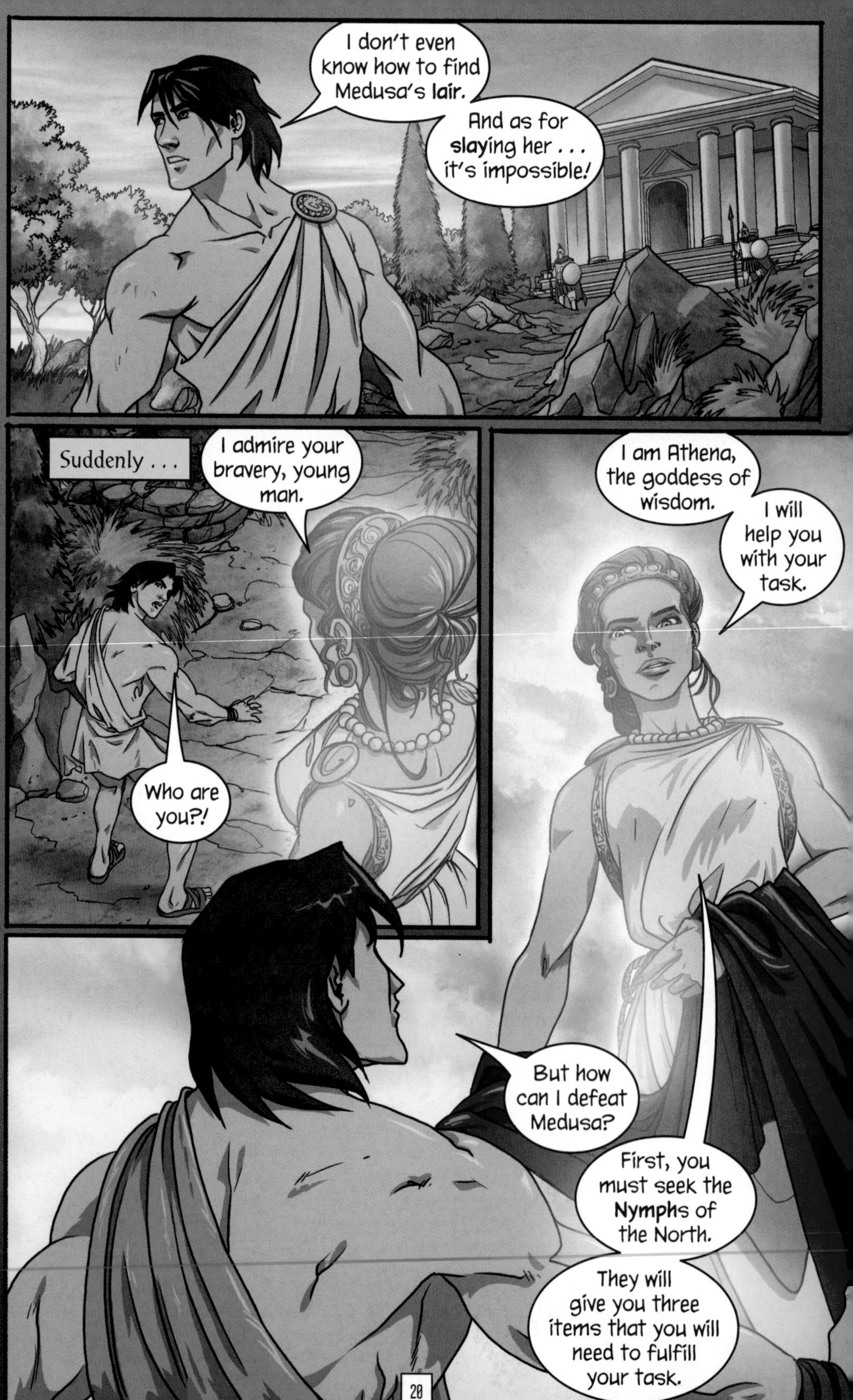

I don't even know how to find Medusa's **lair**.
And as for **slaying** her . . . it's impossible!
Suddenly . . .
I admire your bravery, young man.
Who are you?!
I am Athena, the goddess of wisdom.
I will help you with your task.
But how can I defeat Medusa?
First, you must seek the **Nymphs** of the North.
They will give you three items that you will need to fulfill your task.

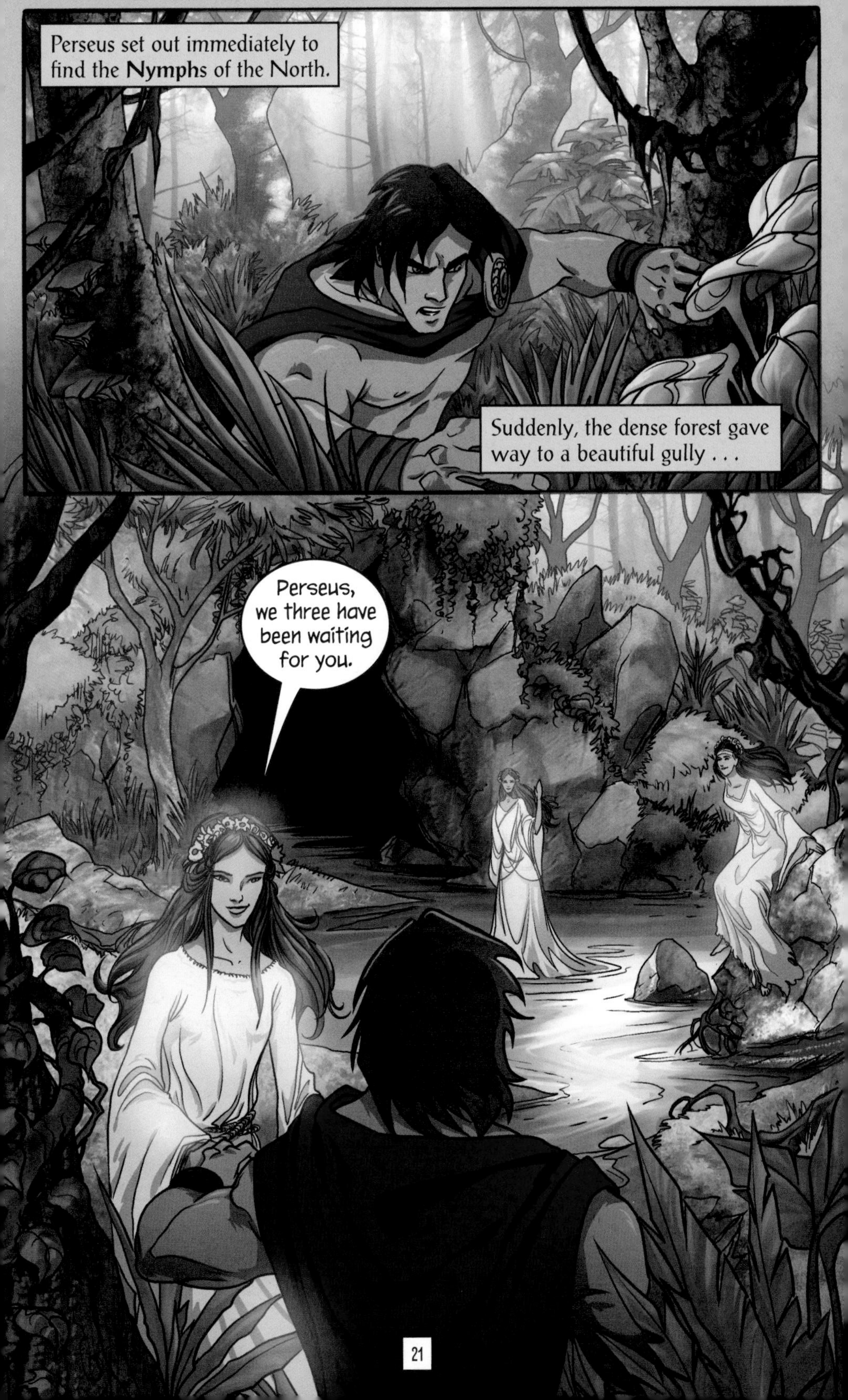
Perseus set out immediately to find the **Nymphs** of the North.
Suddenly, the dense forest gave way to a beautiful gully . . .
Perseus, we three have been waiting for you.

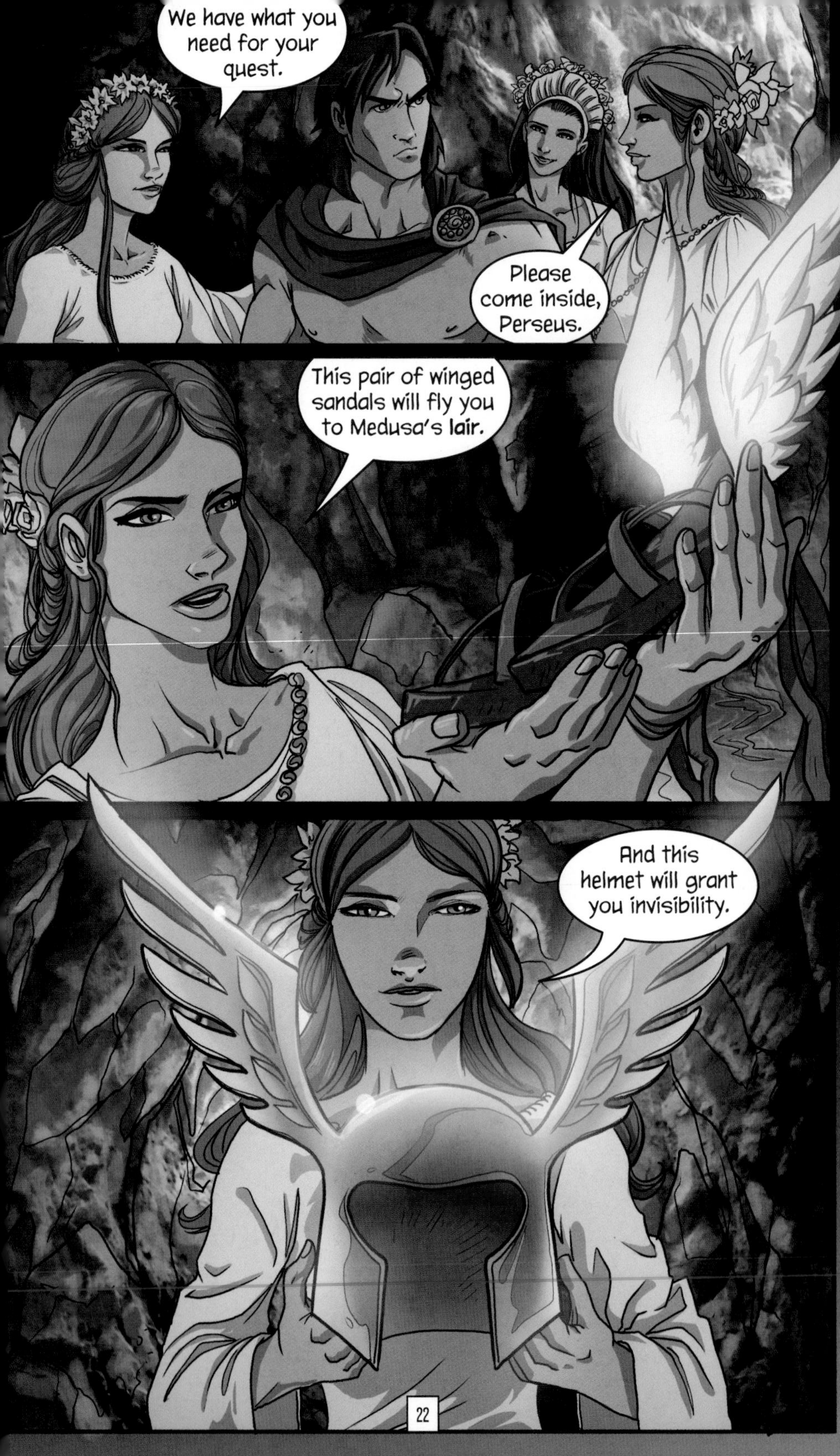
We have what you need for your quest.
Please come inside, Perseus.
This pair of winged sandals will fly you to Medusa's lair.
And this helmet will grant you invisibility.

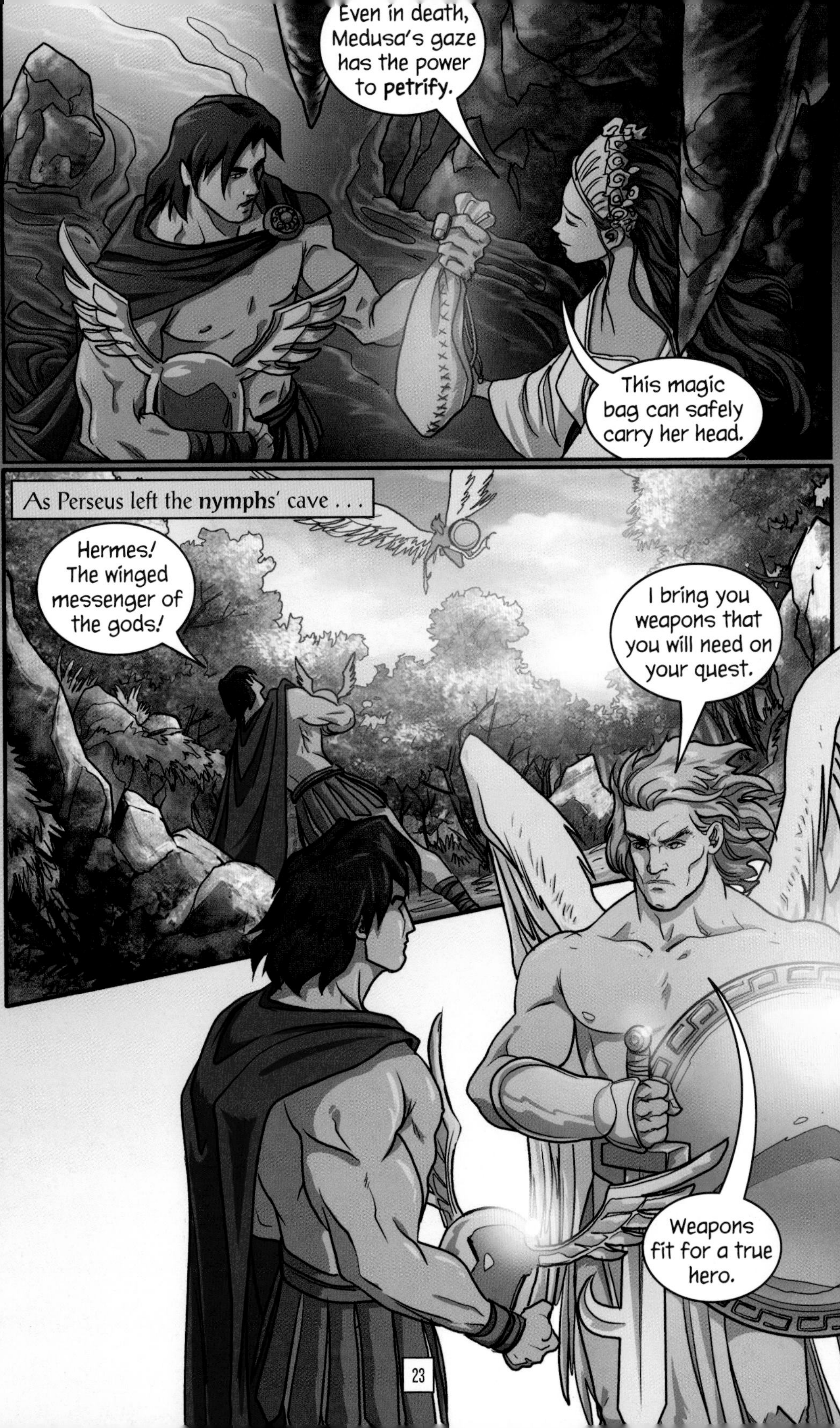
Even in death, Medusa's gaze has the power to petrify.
This magic bag can safely carry her head.
As Perseus left the nymphs' cave . . .
Hermes! The winged messenger of the gods!
I bring you weapons that you will need on your quest.
Weapons fit for a true hero.

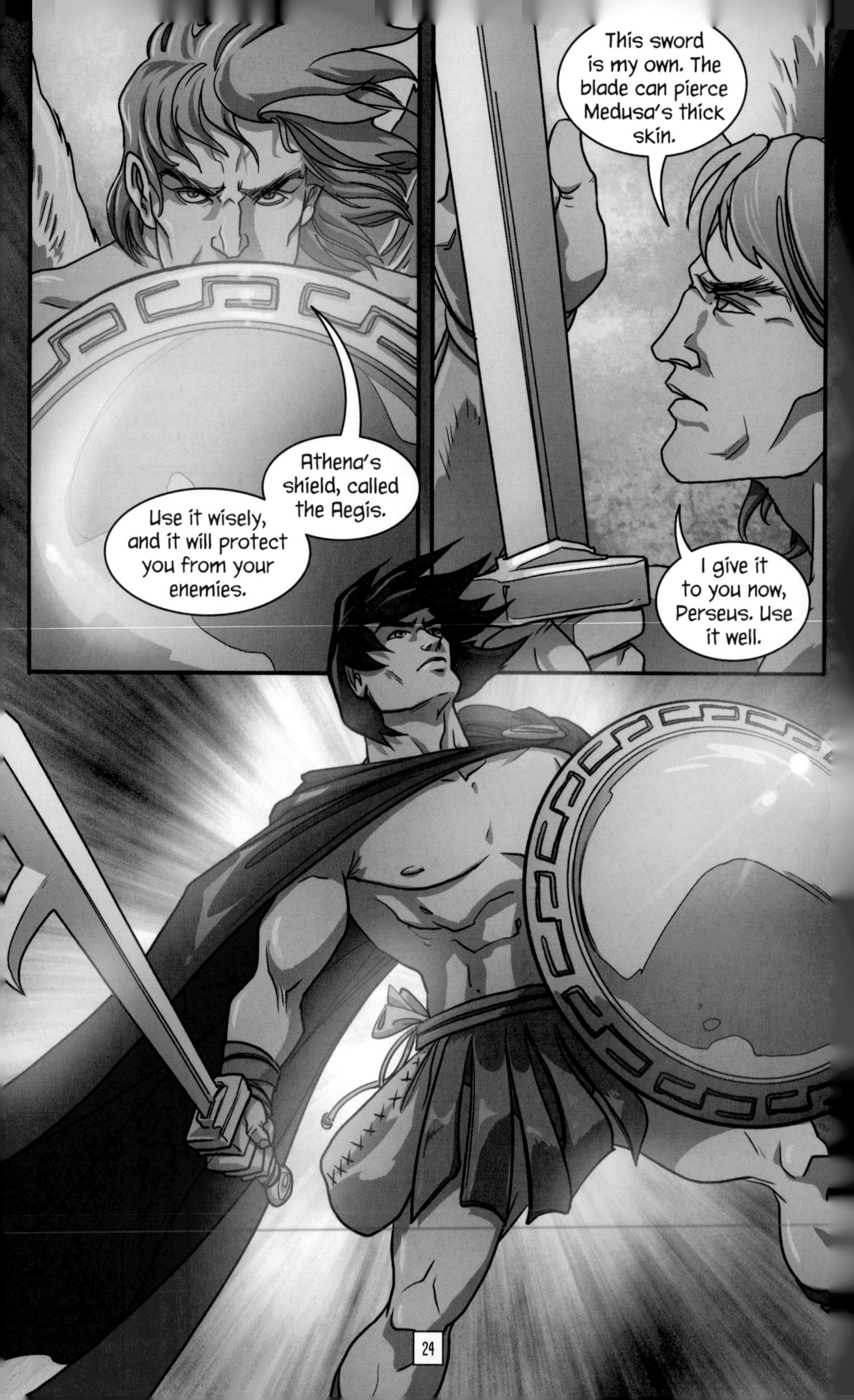
Athena's shield, called the Aegis.
Use it wisely, and it will protect you from your enemies.
This sword is my own. The blade can pierce Medusa's thick skin.
I give it to you now, Perseus. Use it well.

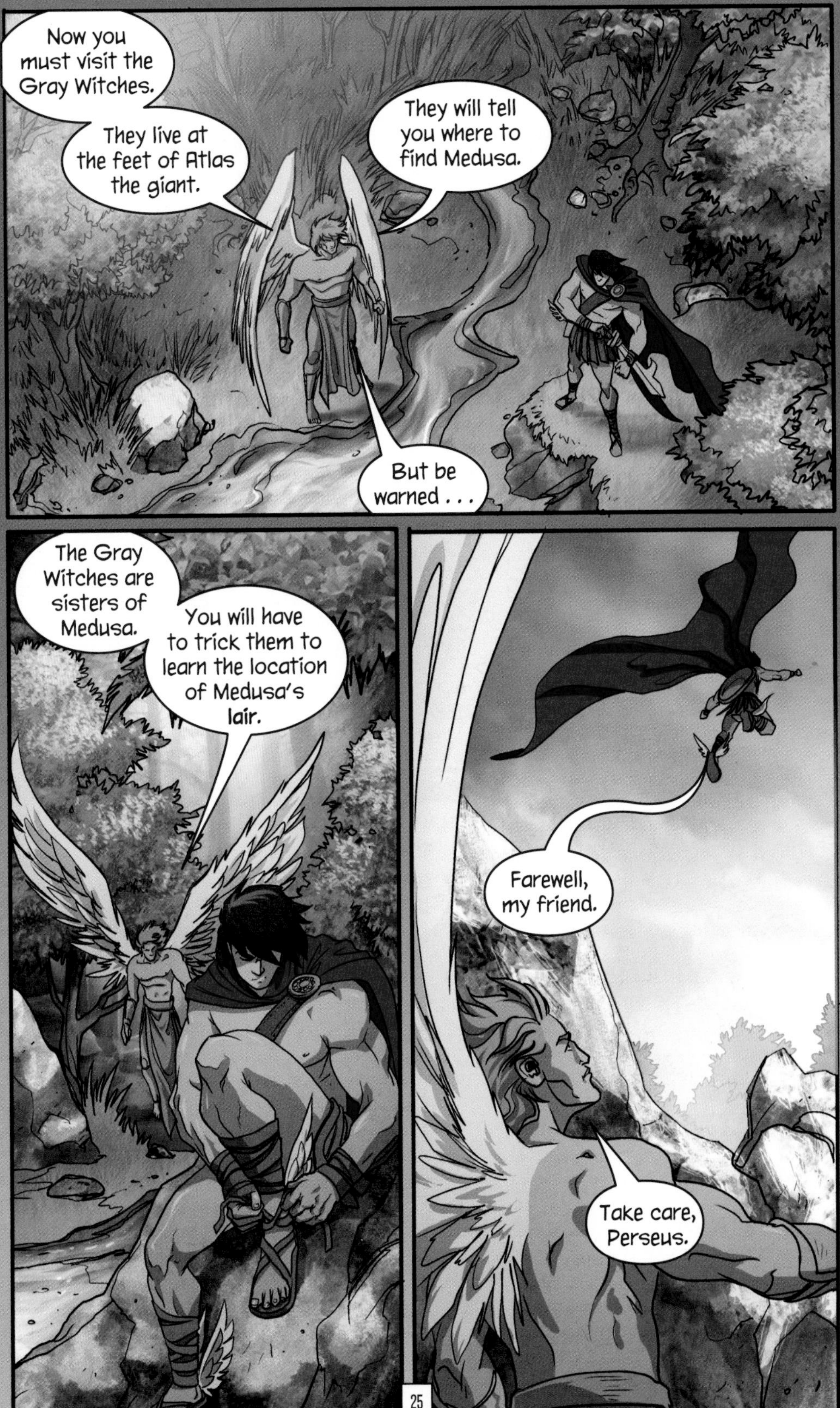
Now you must visit the Gray Witches.
They live at the feet of Atlas the giant.
They will tell you where to find Medusa.
But be warned . . .
The Gray Witches are sisters of Medusa.
You will have to trick them to learn the location of Medusa's lair.
Farewell, my friend.
Take care, Perseus.

CHAPTER 3
# EYE OF THE WITCHES

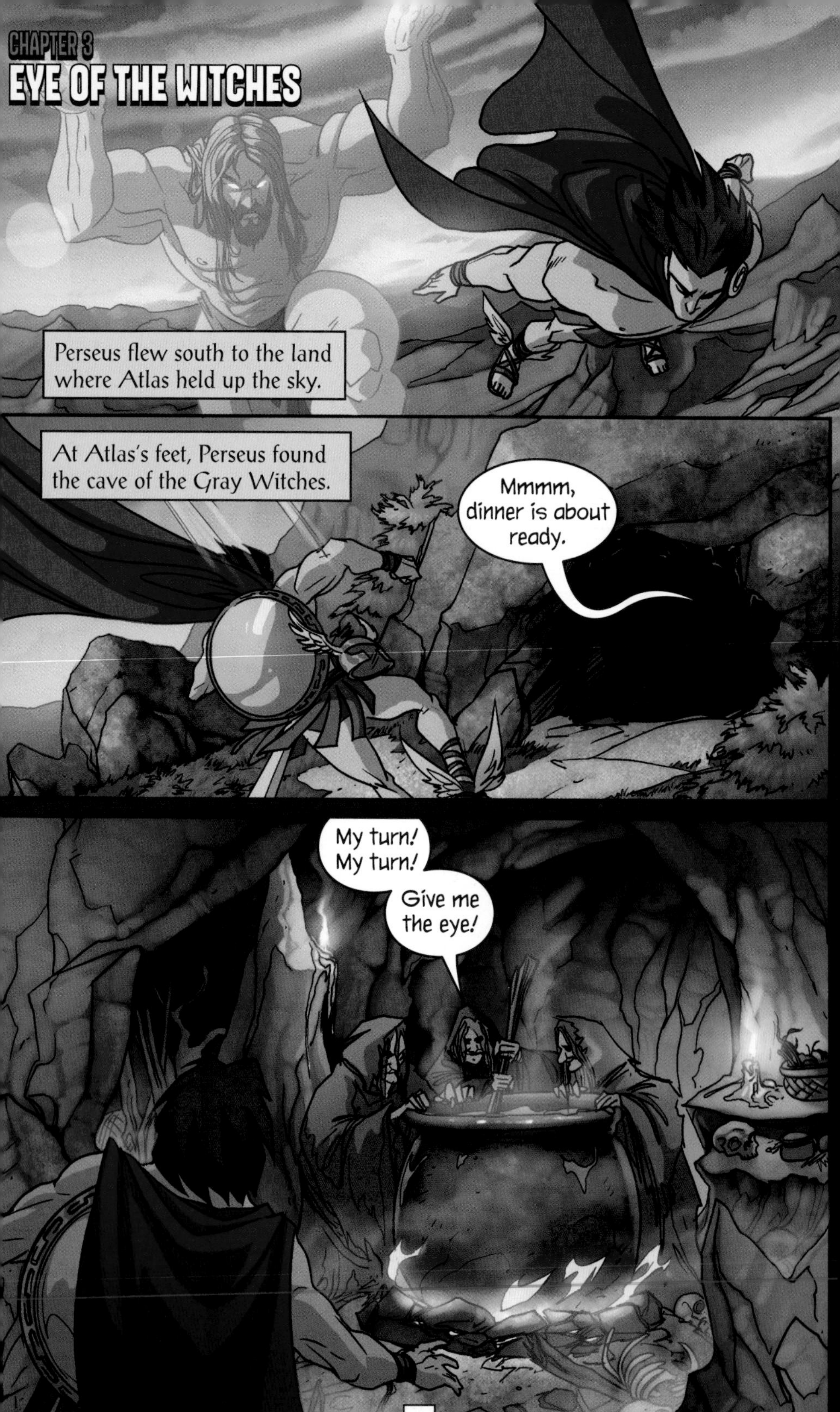

Perseus flew south to the land where Atlas held up the sky.
At Atlas's feet, Perseus found the cave of the Gray Witches.
Mmmm, dinner is about ready.
My turn! My turn!
Give me the eye!

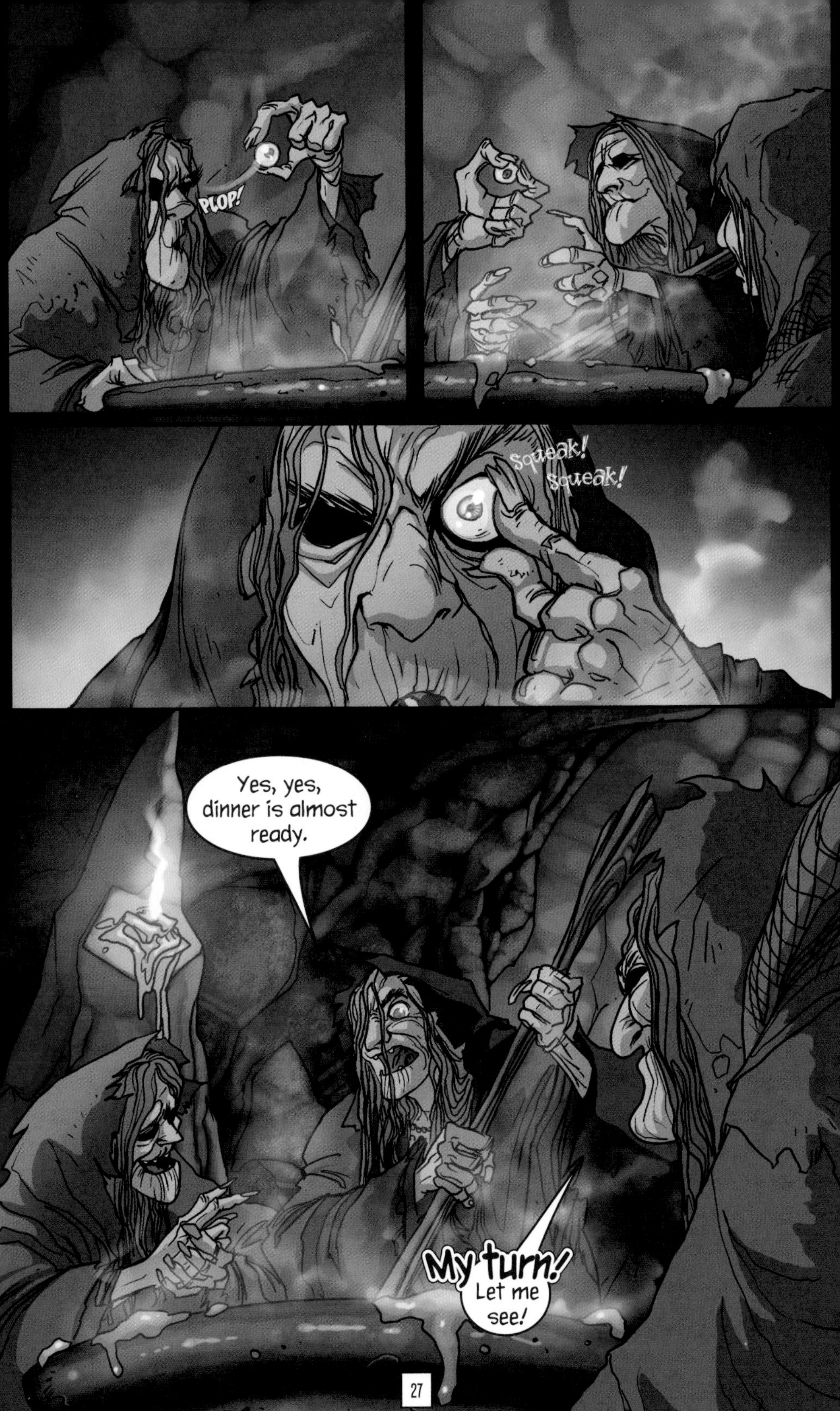
PLOP!
Squeak!
Squeak!
Yes, yes, dinner is almost ready.
My turn! Let me see!

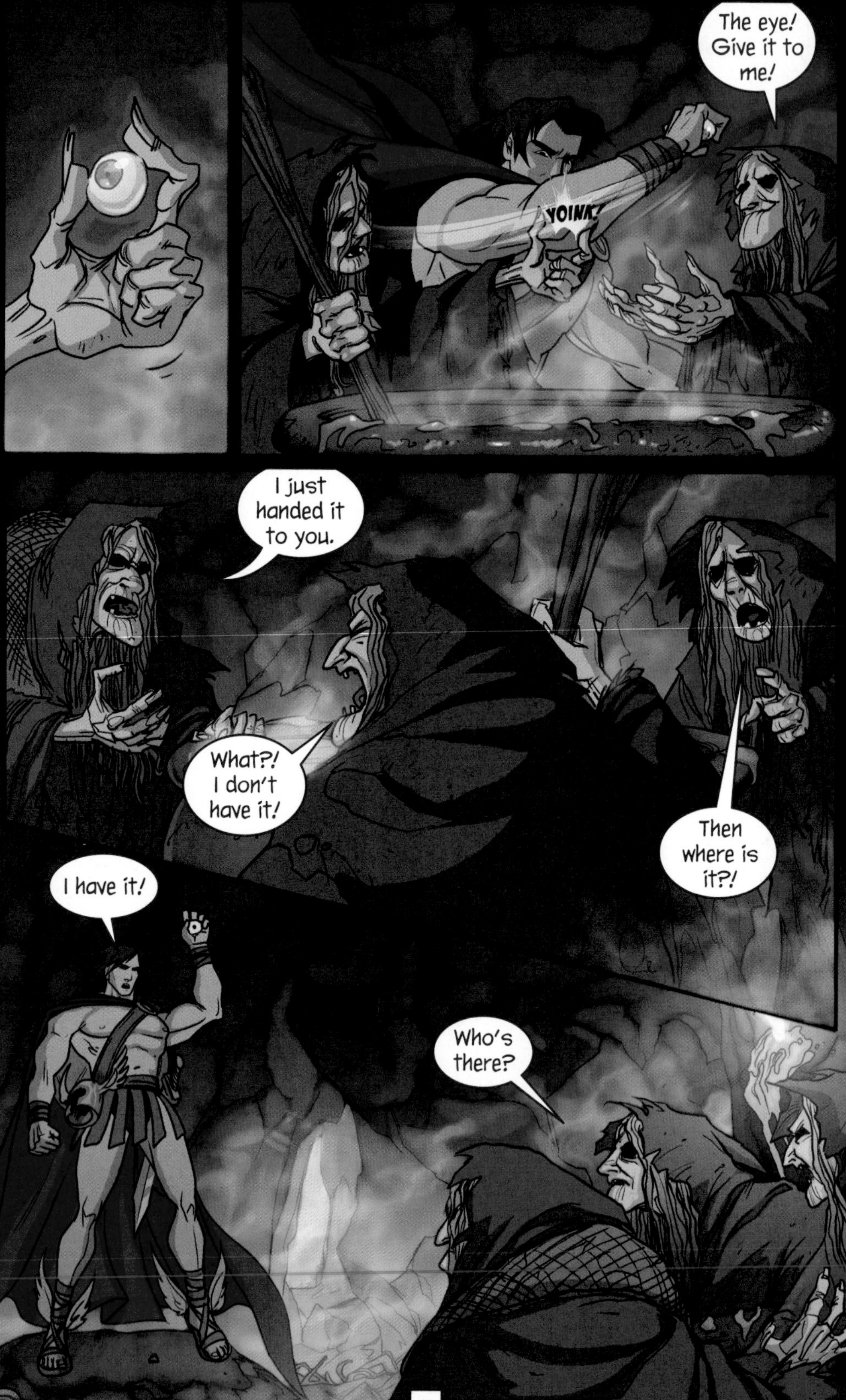
The eye! Give it to me!
YOINK!
I just handed it to you.
What?! I don't have it!
Then where is it?!
I have it!
Who's there?

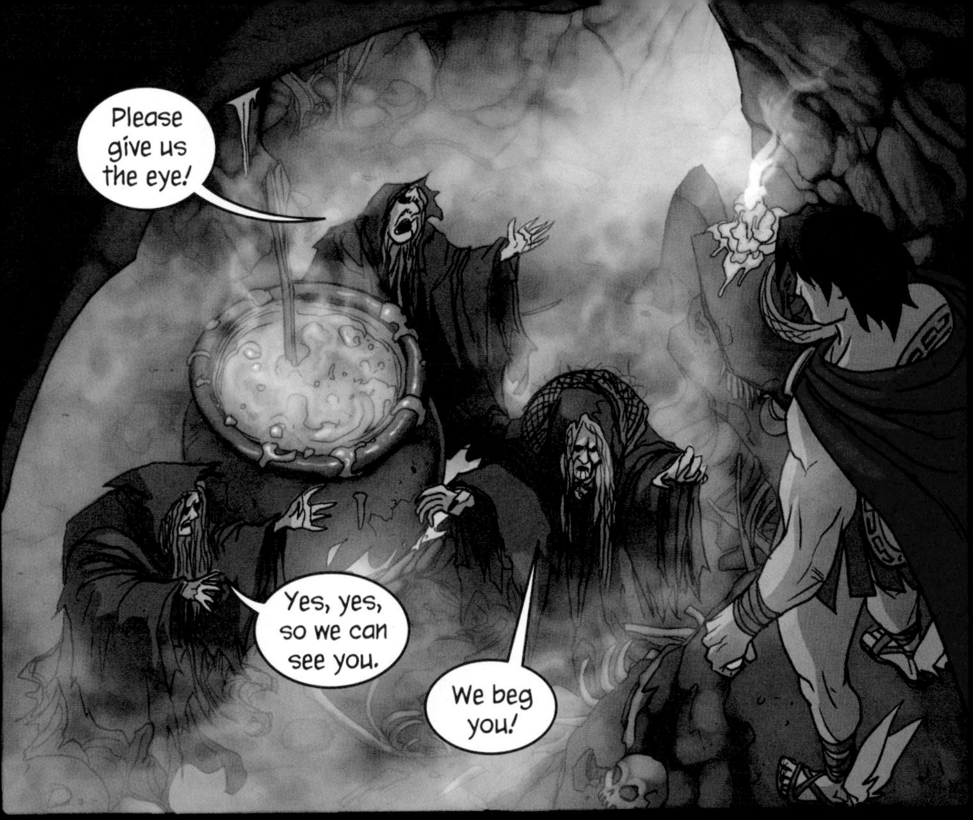
Please give us the eye!
Yes, yes, so we can see you.
We beg you!

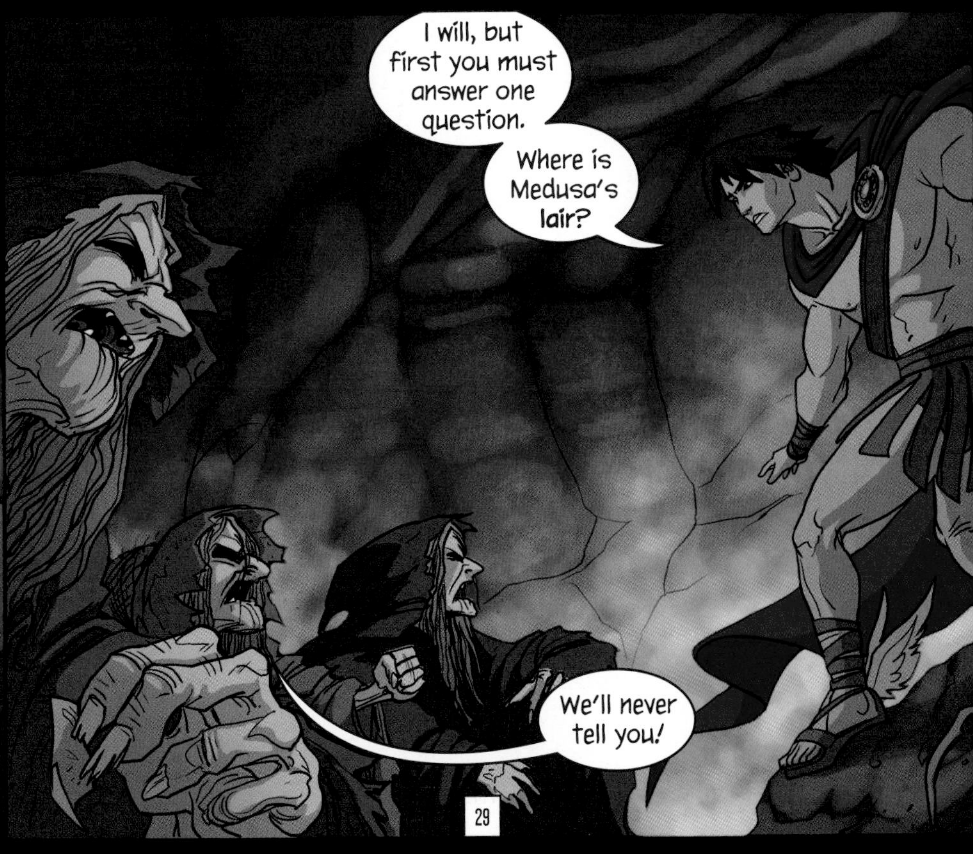
I will, but first you must answer one question.
Where is Medusa's **lair?**
We'll never tell you!

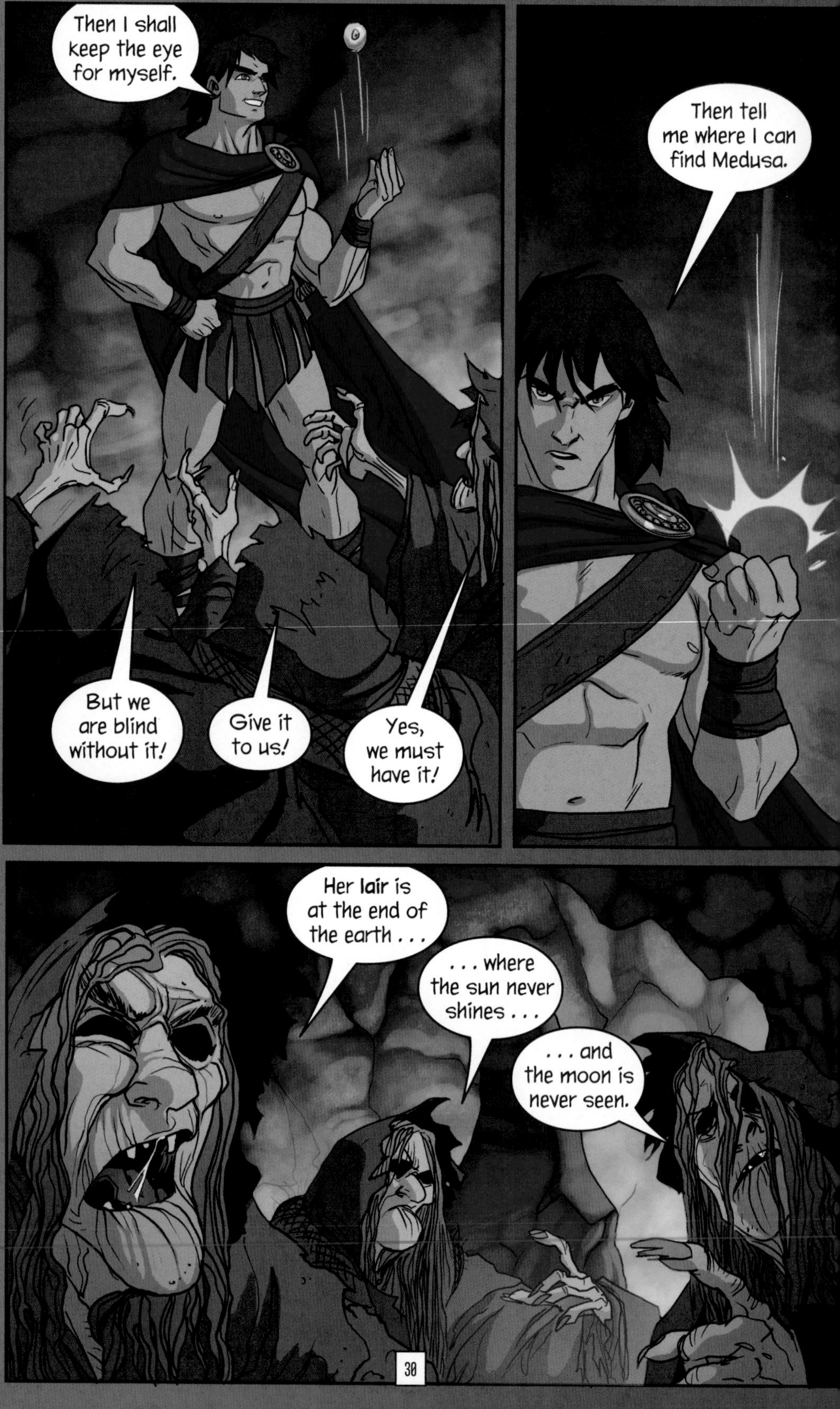
Then I shall keep the eye for myself.
But we are blind without it!
Give it to us!
Yes, we must have it!
Then tell me where I can find Medusa.
Her **lair** is at the end of the earth . . .
. . . where the sun never shines . . .
. . . and the moon is never seen.

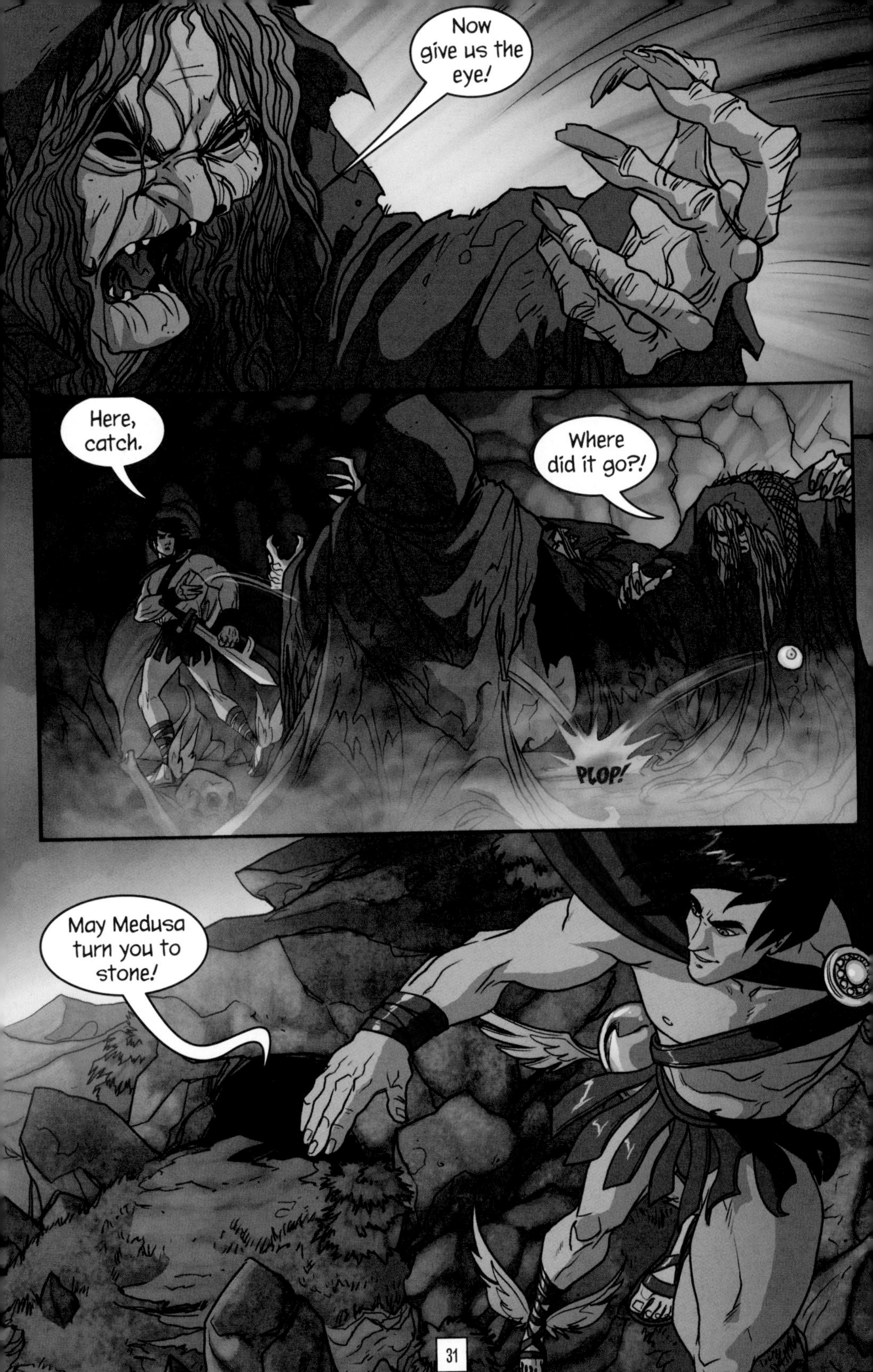
Now give us the eye!
Here, catch.
Where did it go?!
PLOP!
May Medusa turn you to stone!

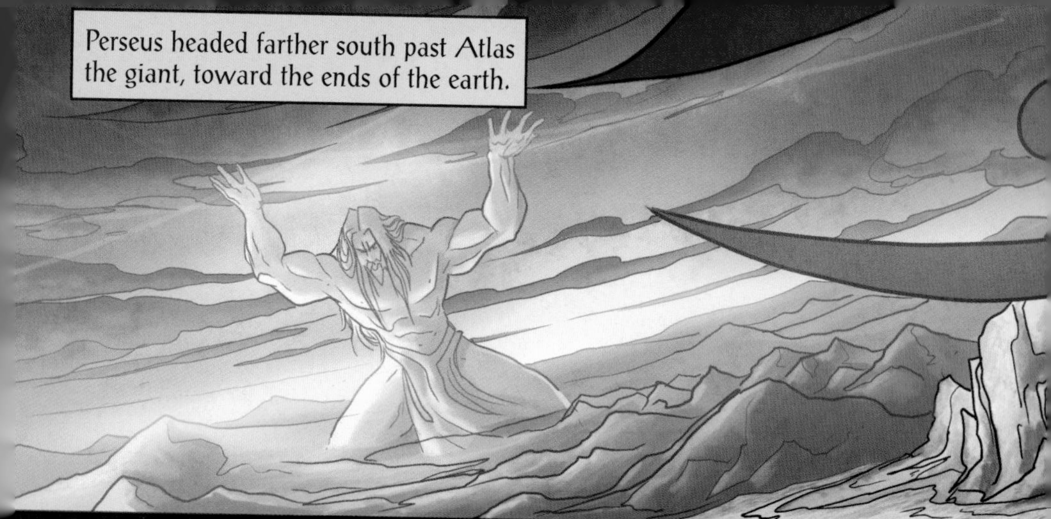
Perseus headed farther south past Atlas the giant, toward the ends of the earth.

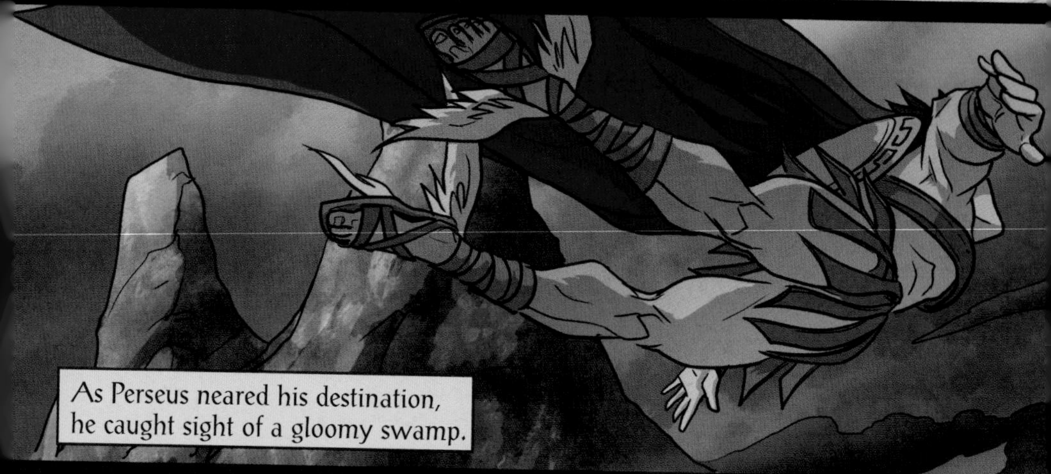
As Perseus neared his destination, he caught sight of a gloomy swamp.

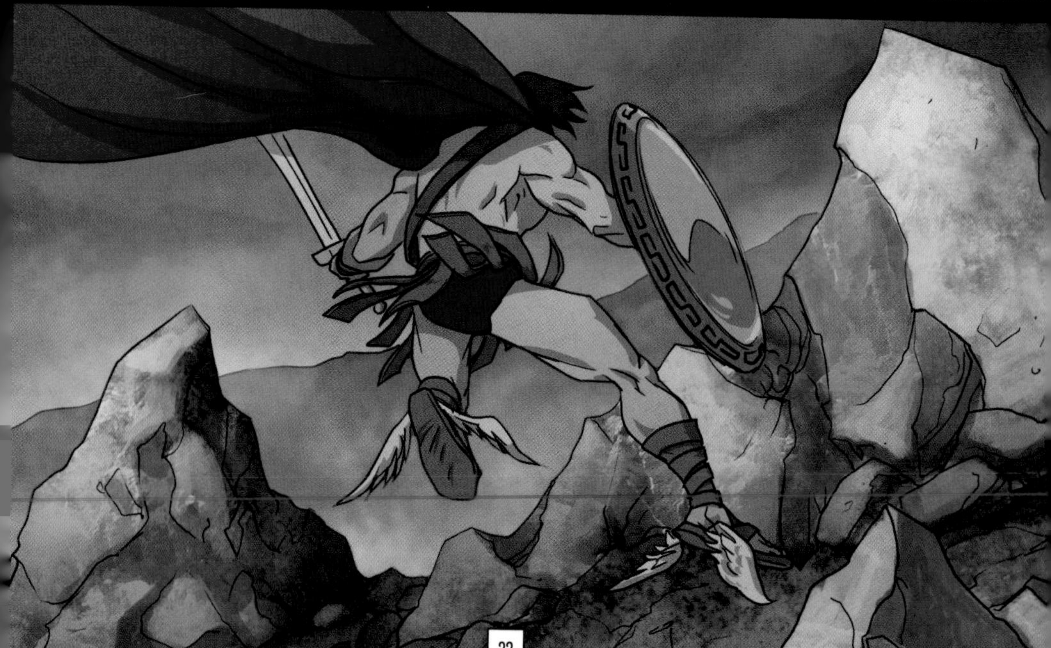

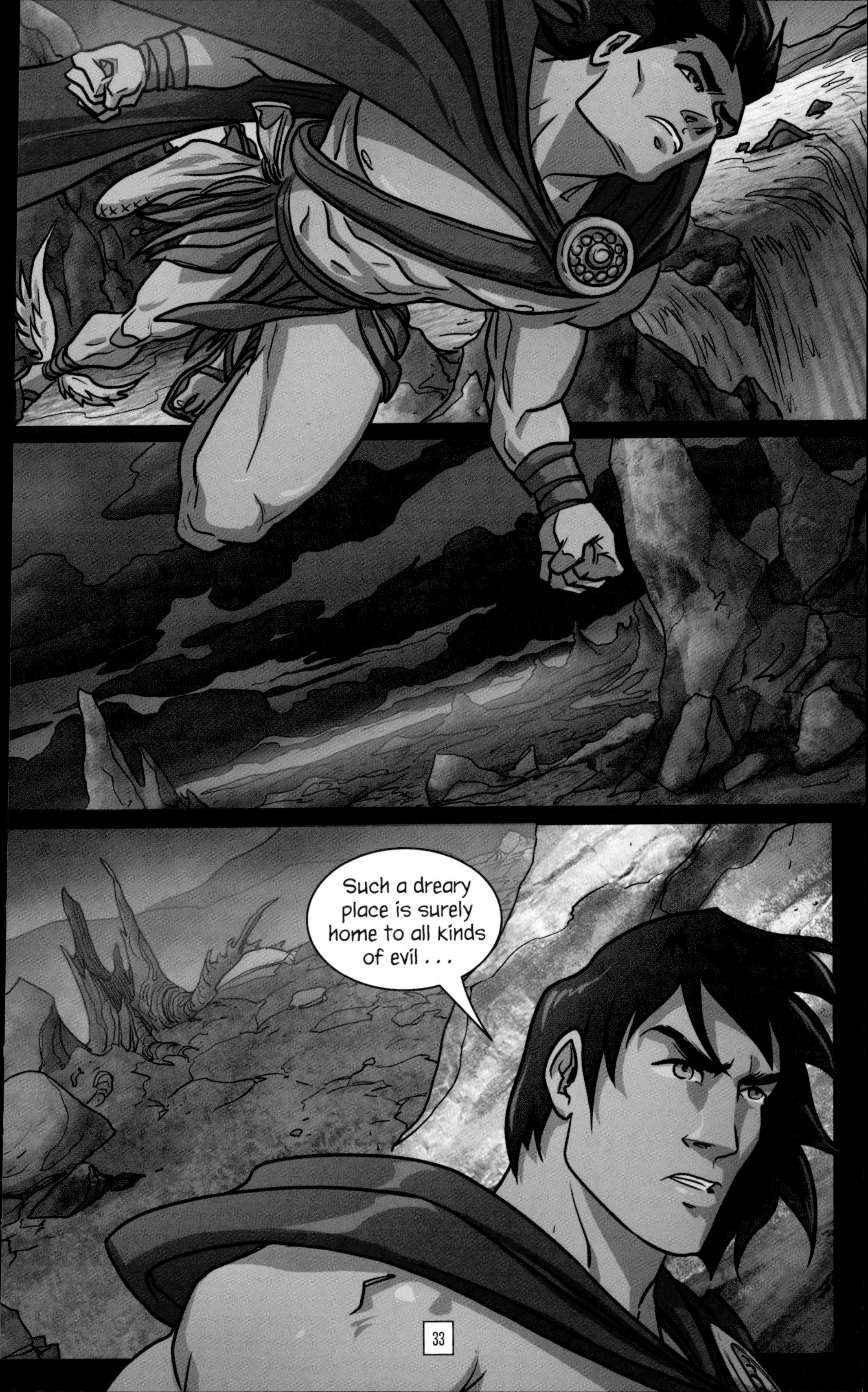
Such a dreary place is surely home to all kinds of evil . . .

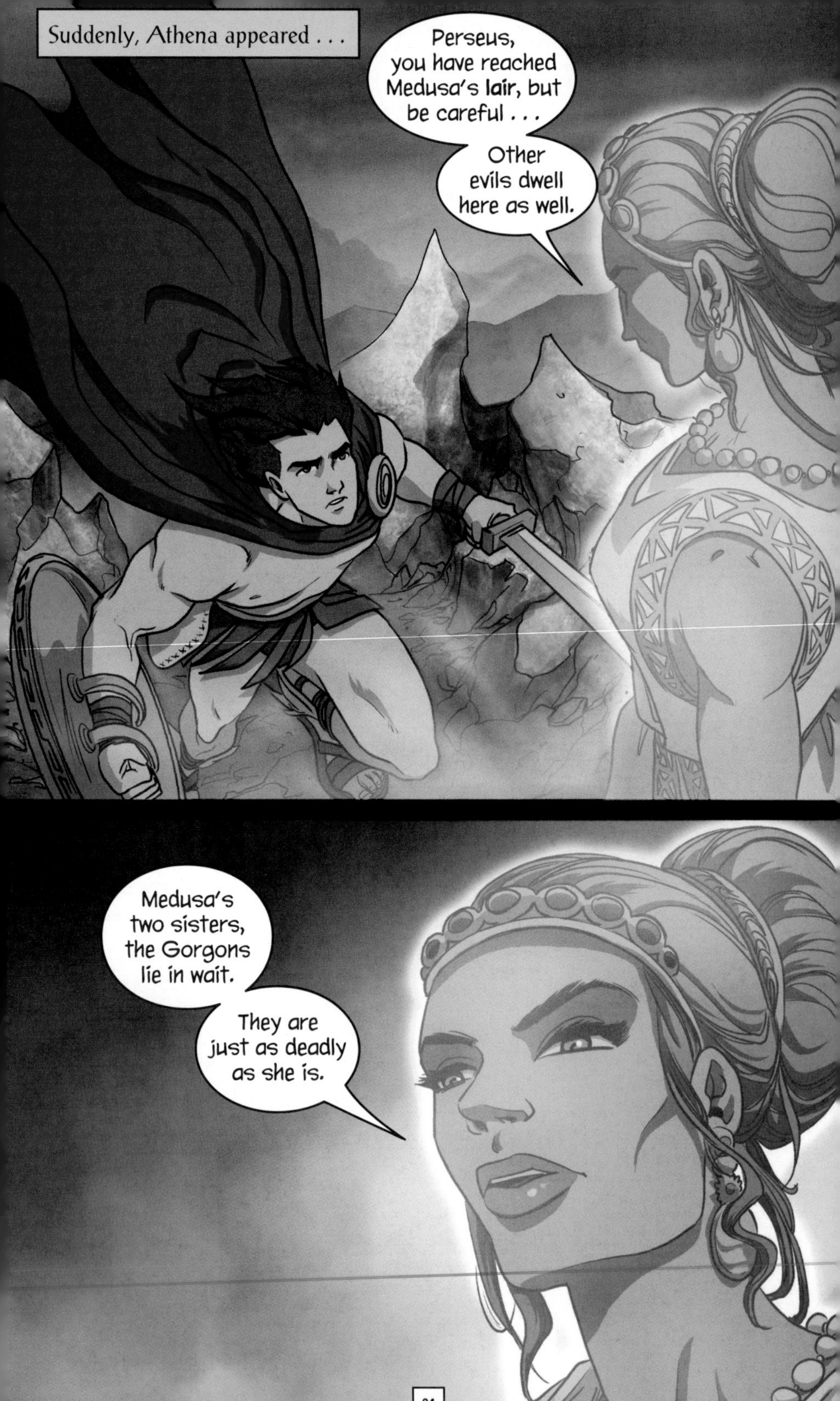
Suddenly, Athena appeared . . .
Perseus, you have reached Medusa's lair, but be careful . . .
Other evils dwell here as well.
Medusa's two sisters, the Gorgons lie in wait.
They are just as deadly as she is.

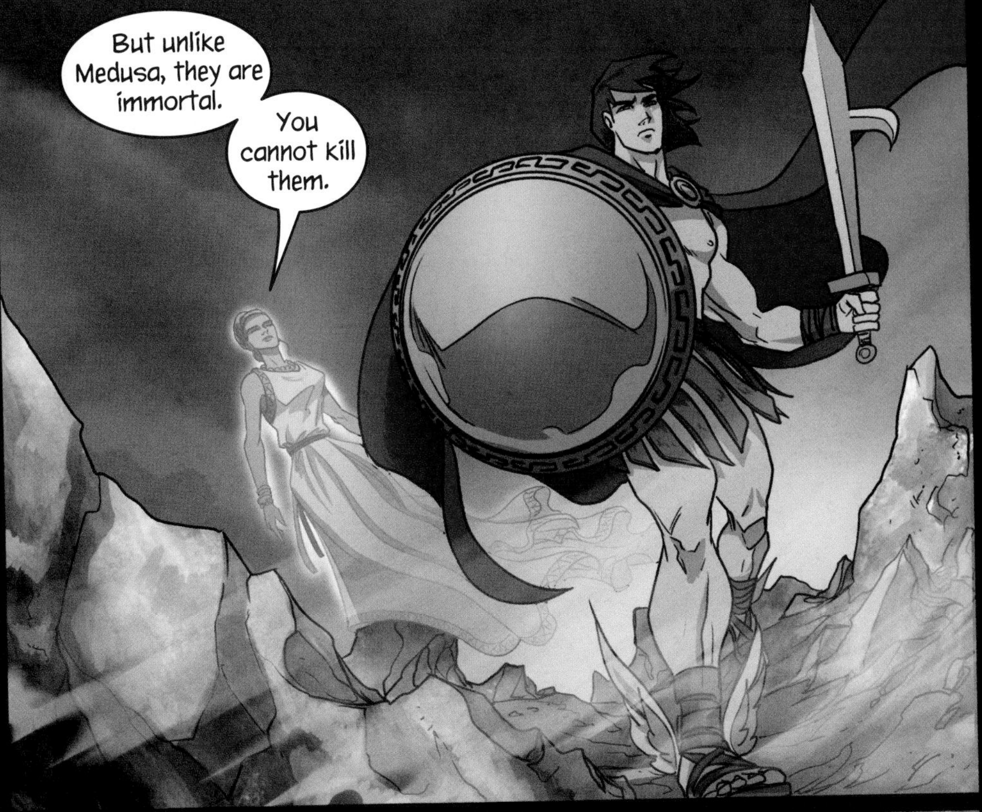
But unlike Medusa, they are immortal.
You cannot kill them.

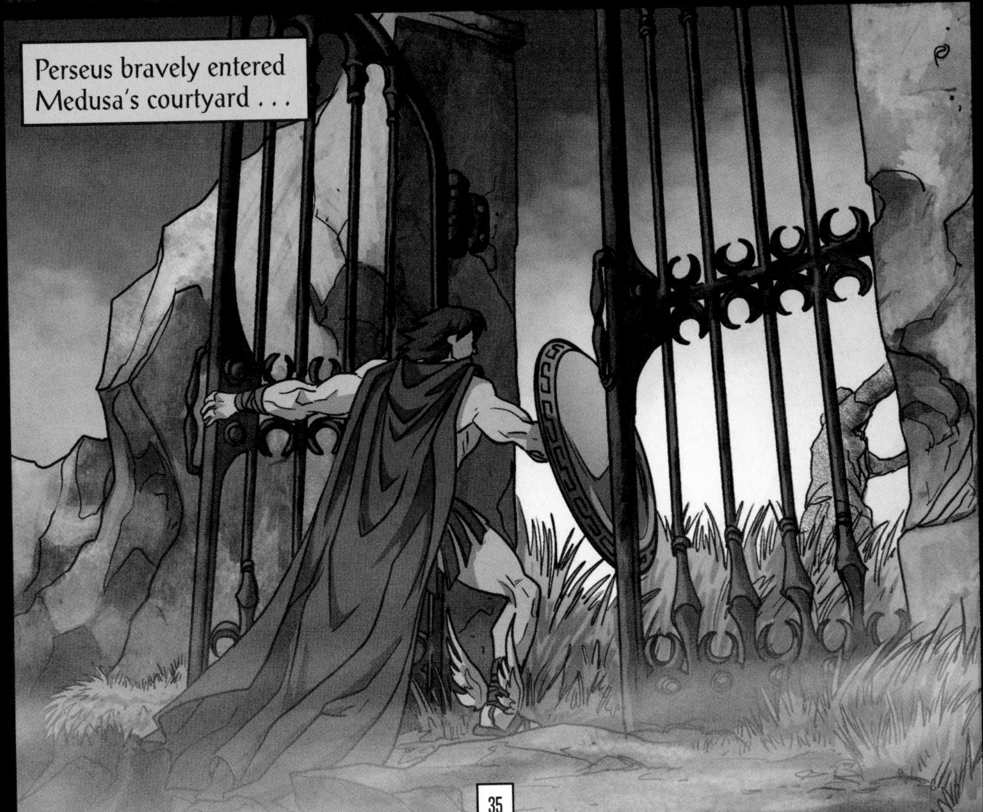
Perseus bravely entered Medusa's courtyard . . .

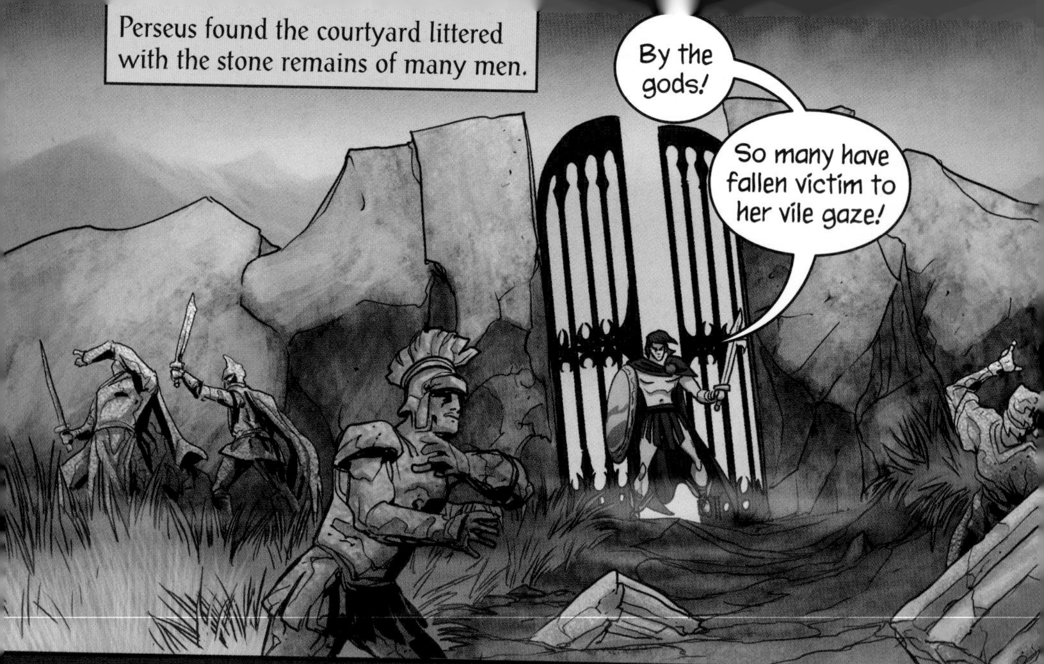
Perseus found the courtyard littered with the stone remains of many men.
By the gods!
So many have fallen victim to her vile gaze!

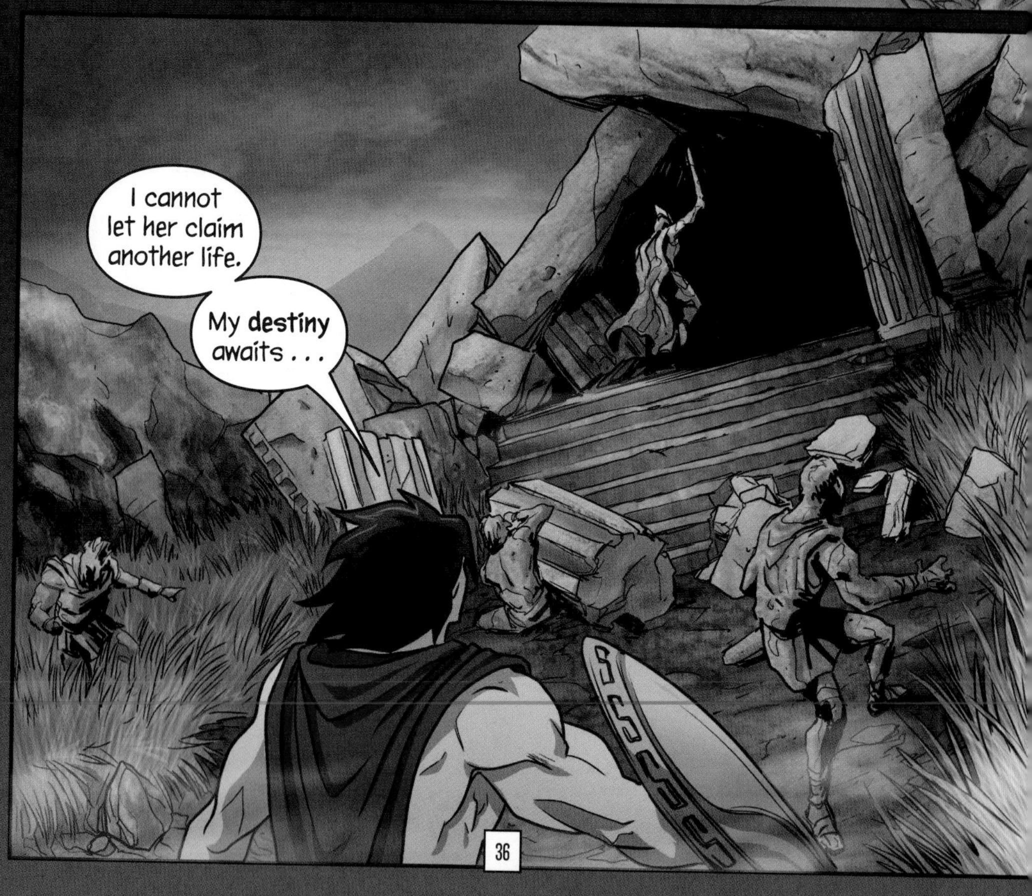
I cannot let her claim another life.
My **destiny** awaits . . .

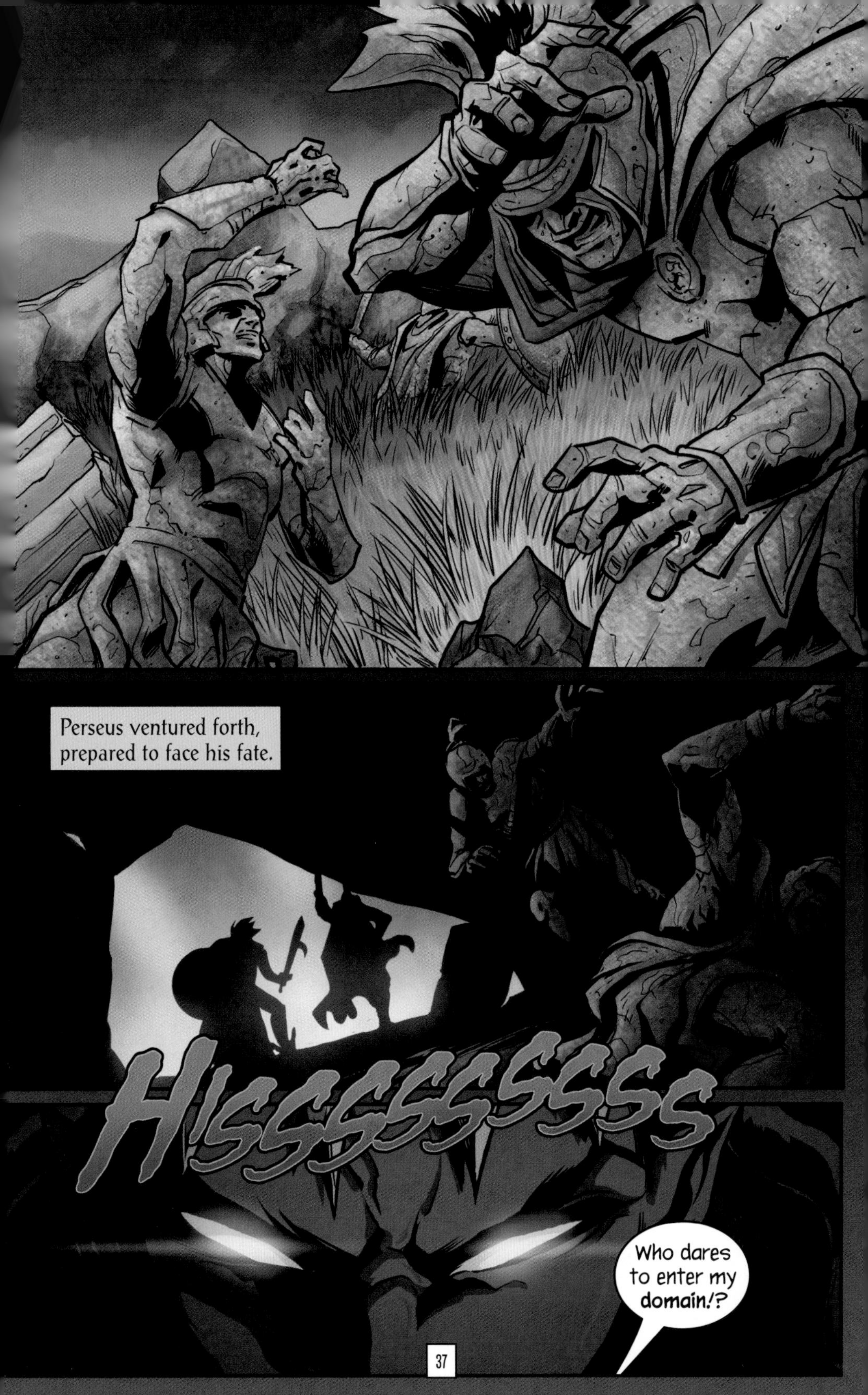
Perseus ventured forth,
prepared to face his fate.
HISSSSSSSSS
Who dares
to enter my
domain!?

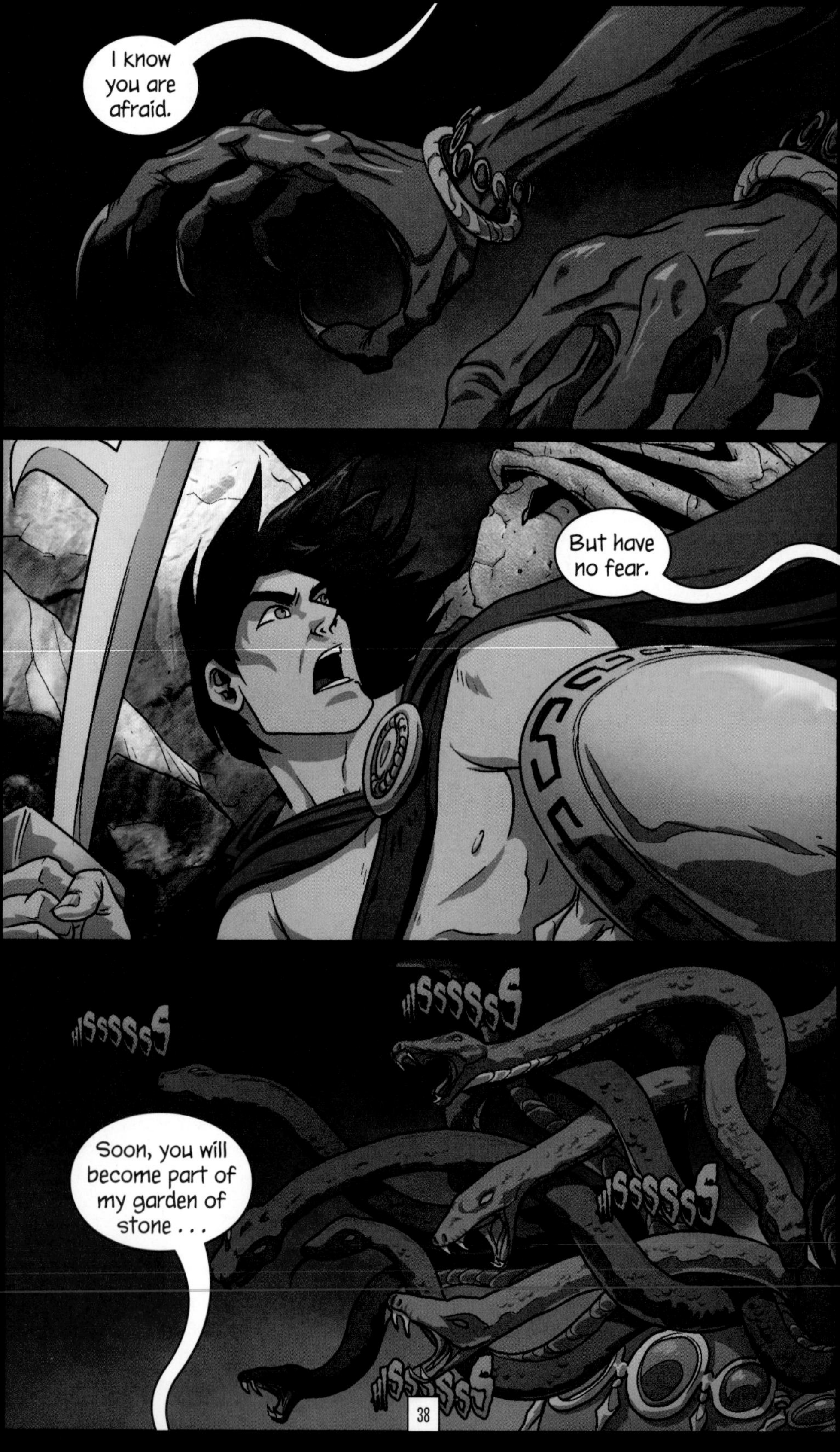
I know you are afraid.
But have no fear.
HISSSSSS
HISSSSSS
Soon, you will become part of my garden of stone . . .
HISSSSSS
HISSSSSS

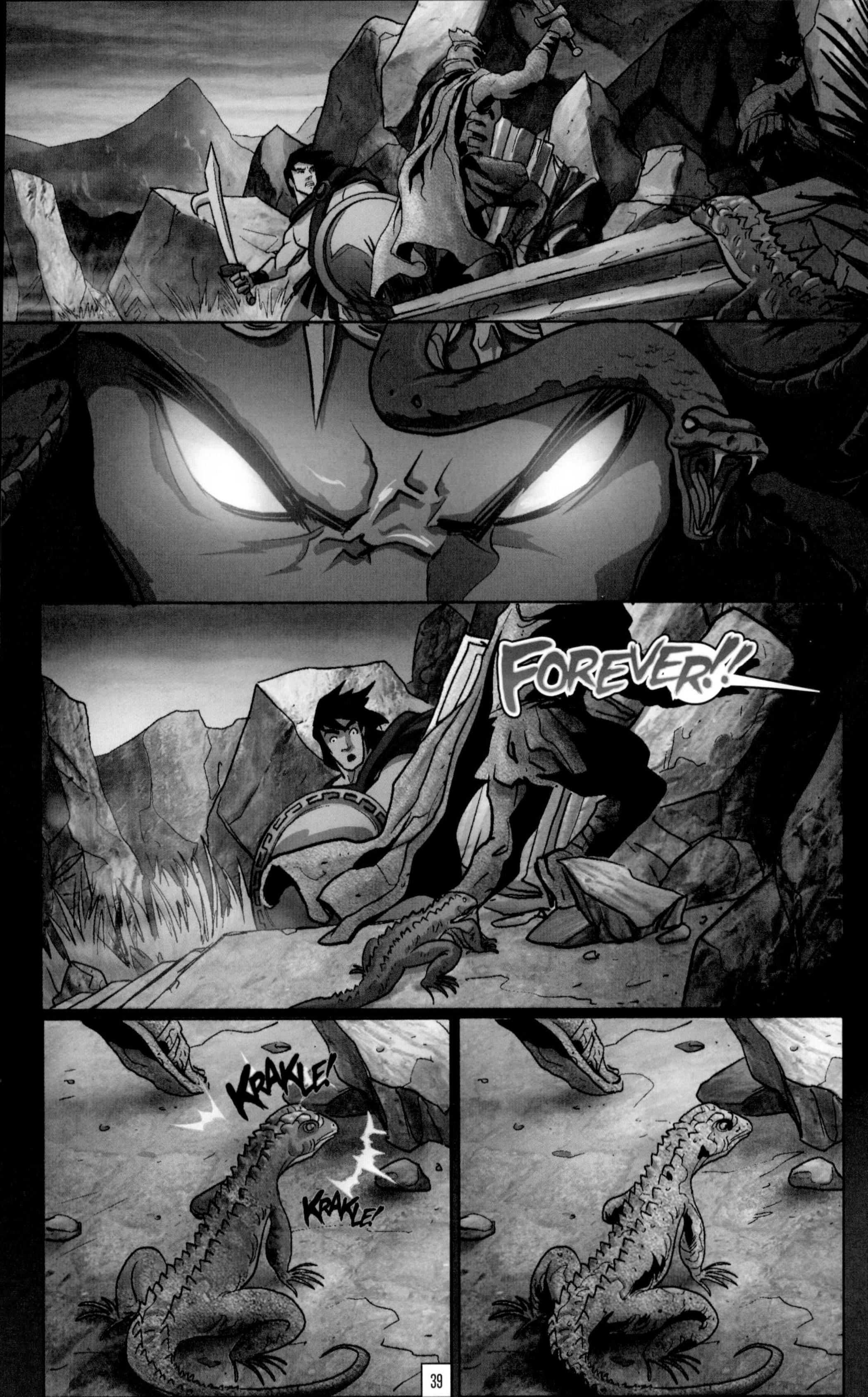
FOREVER!!
KRAKLE!
KRAKLE!

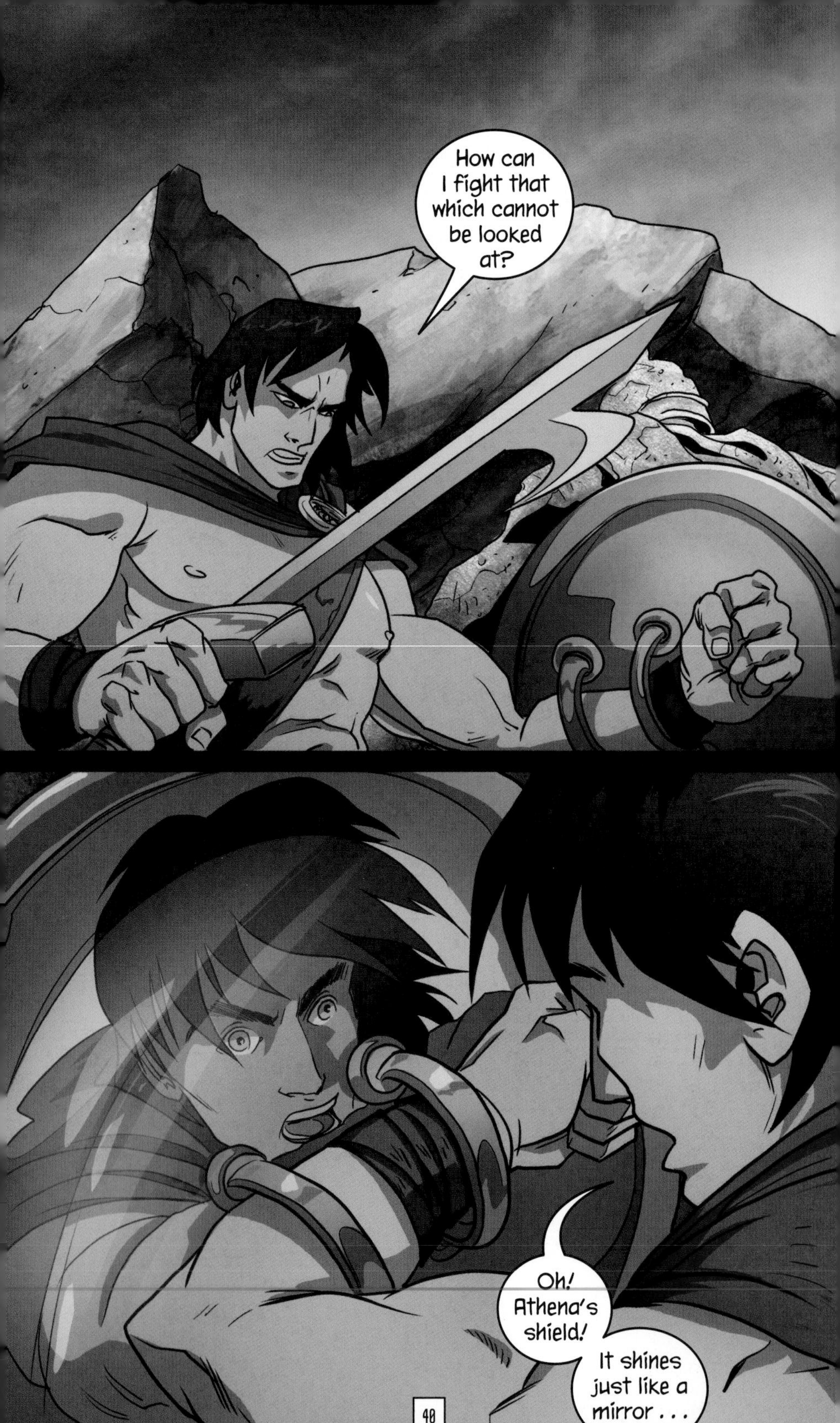
How can I fight that which cannot be looked at?
Oh! Athena's shield!
It shines just like a mirror . . .

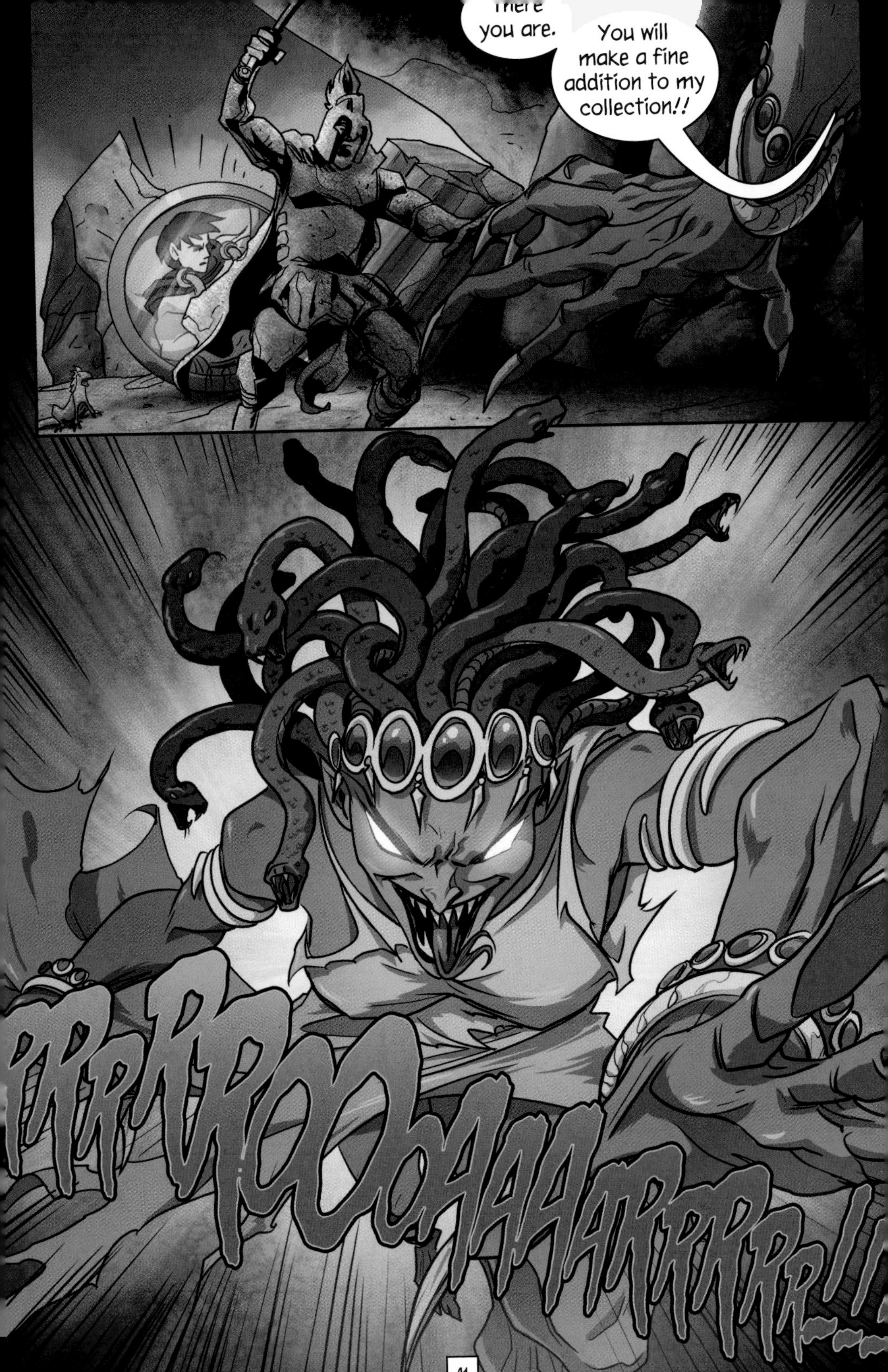
you are.
You will make a fine addition to my collection!!
RRRROOOAAAARRRRR!!...

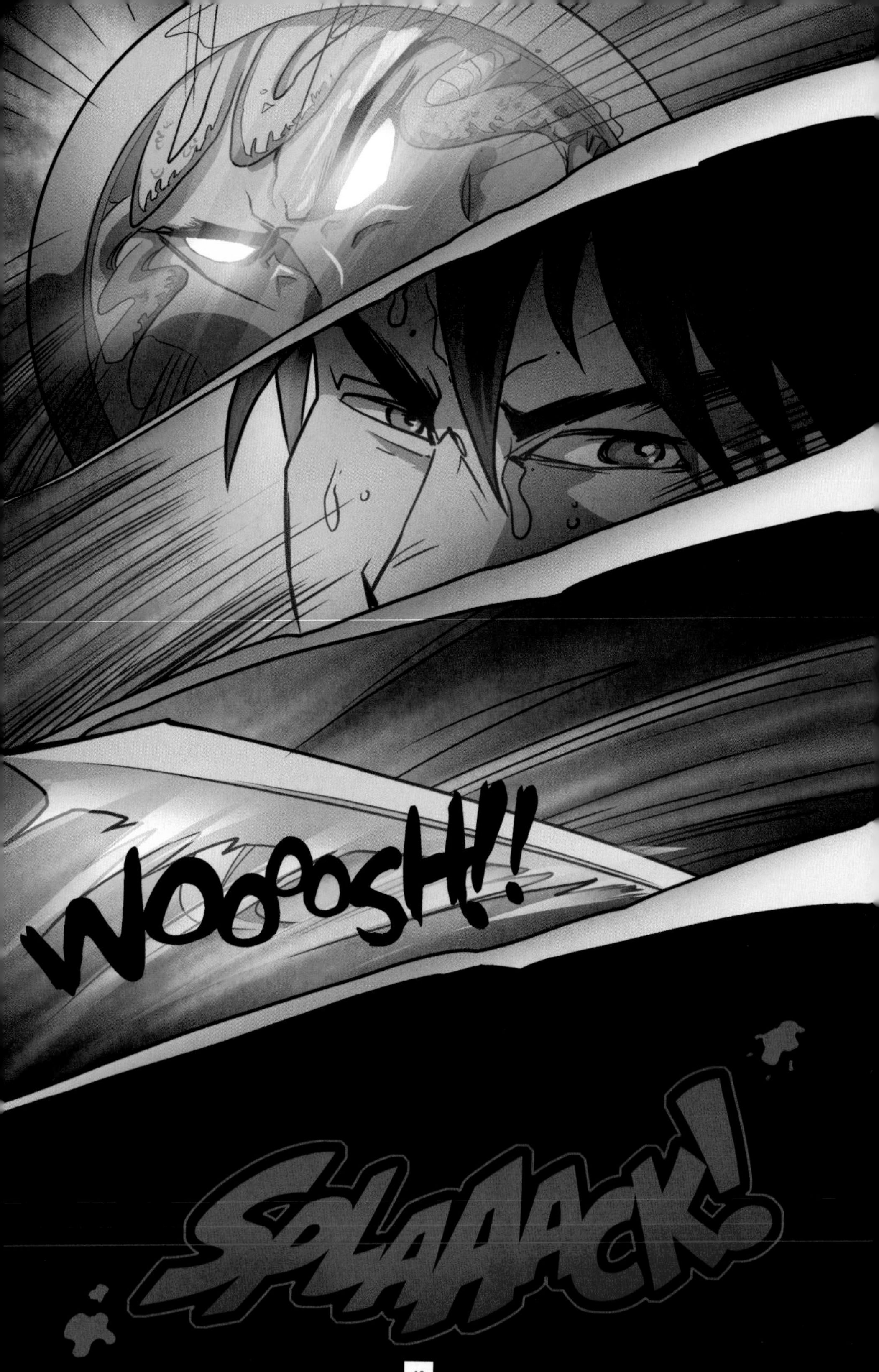
WOOOOSH!!
SPLAAACK!

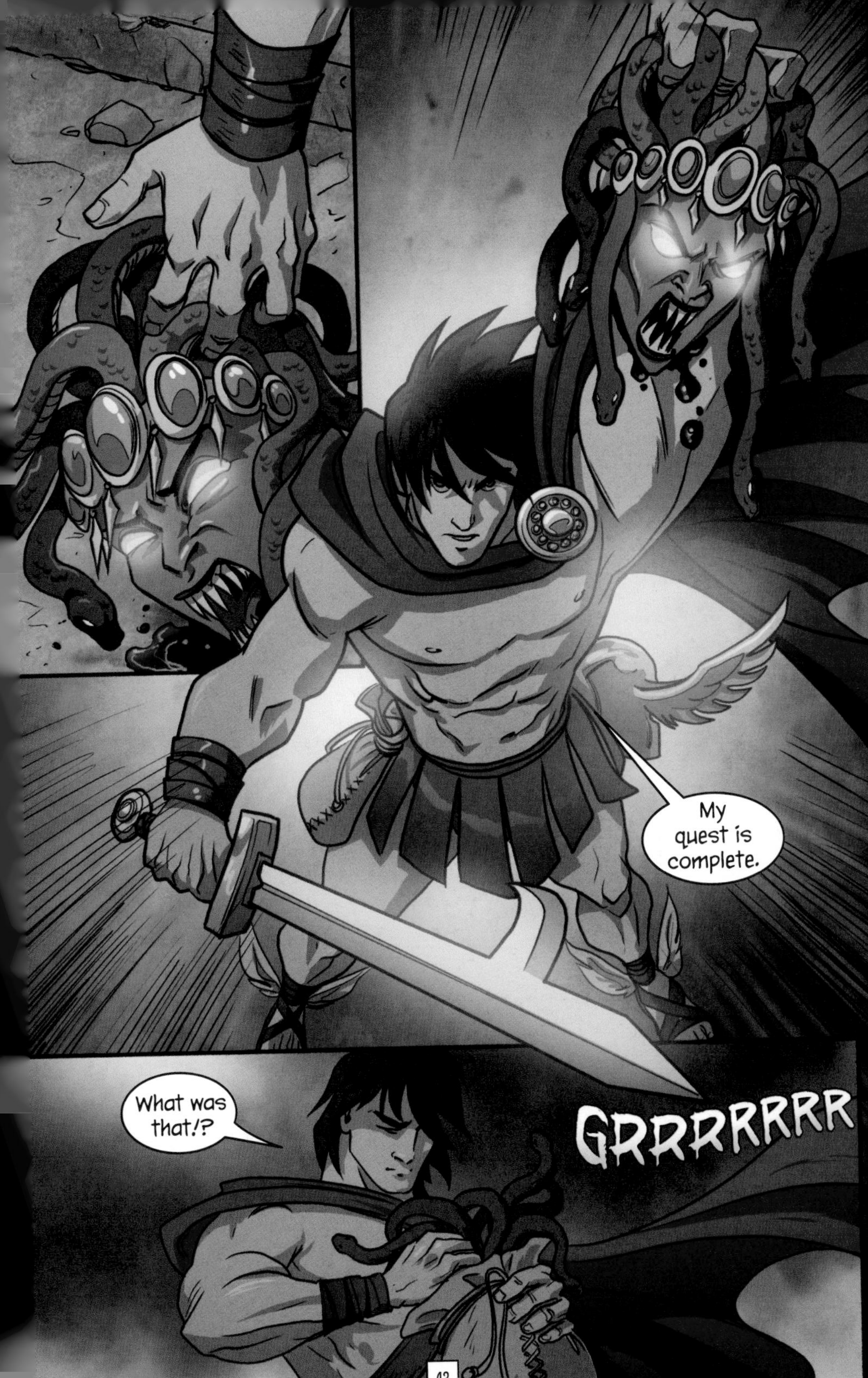
My quest is complete.
GRRRRRRR
What was that!?

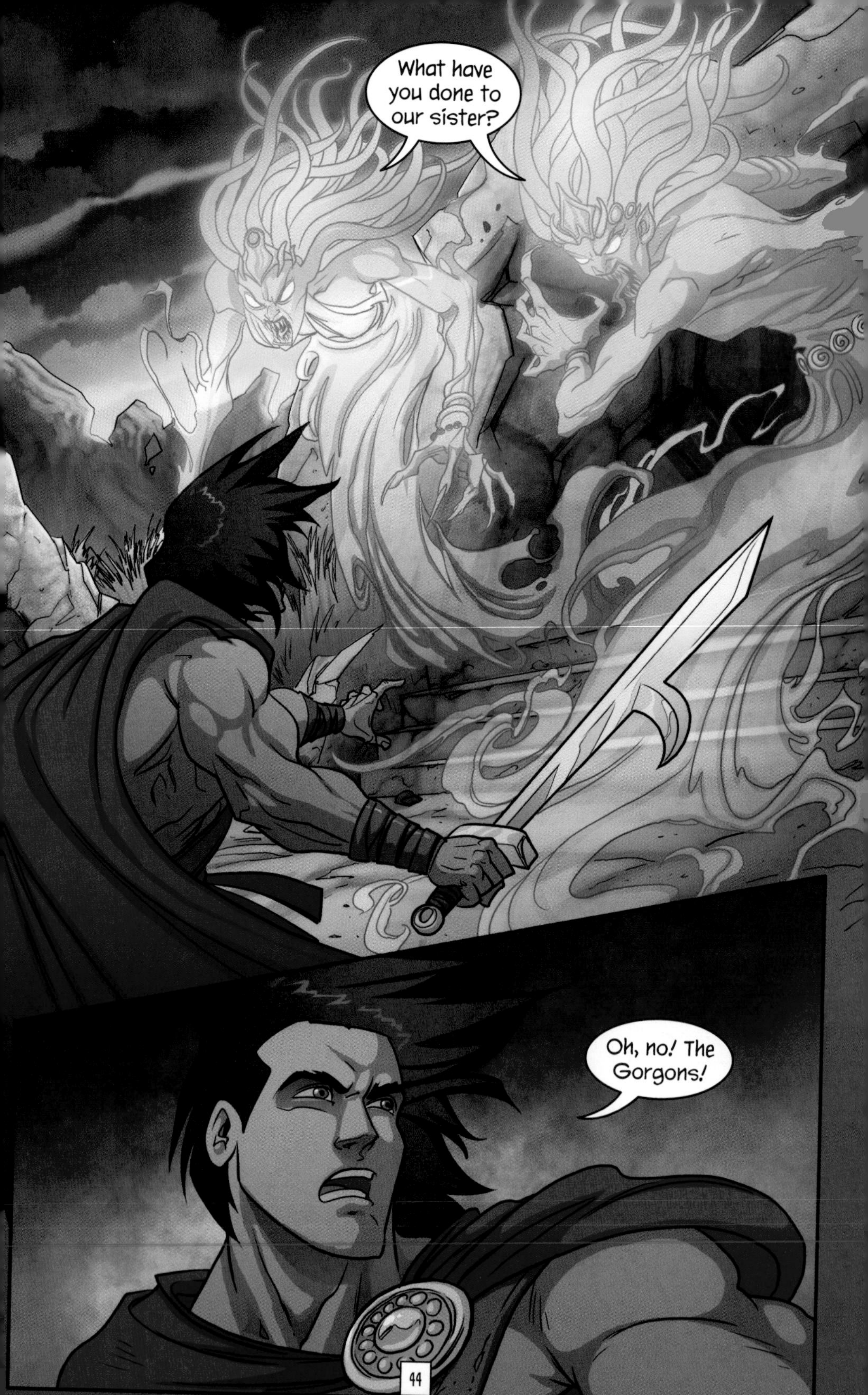
What have you done to our sister?
Oh, no! The Gorgons!

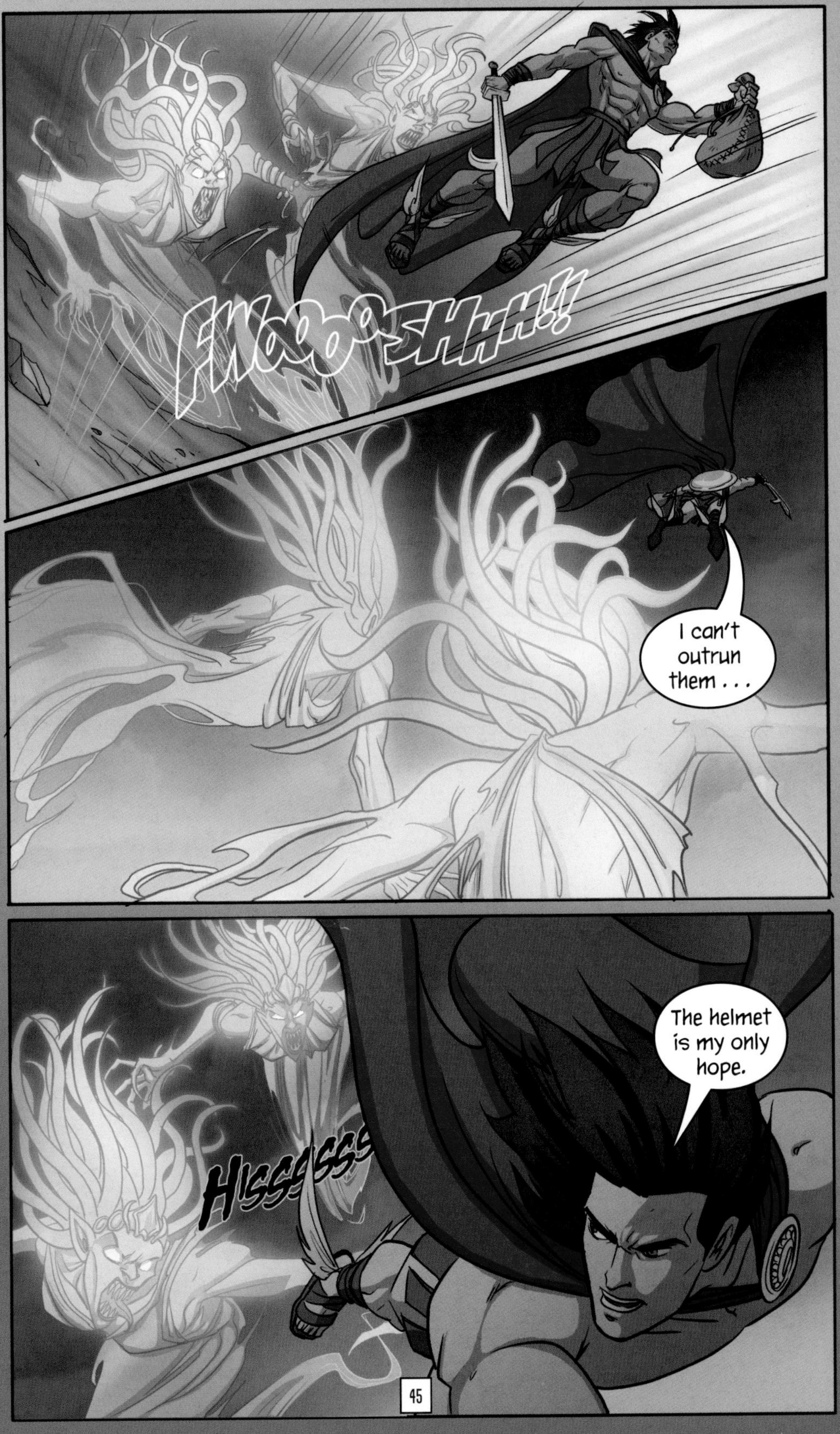
FWOOOSHHH!!
I can't outrun them . . .
The helmet is my only hope.
HISSSSS

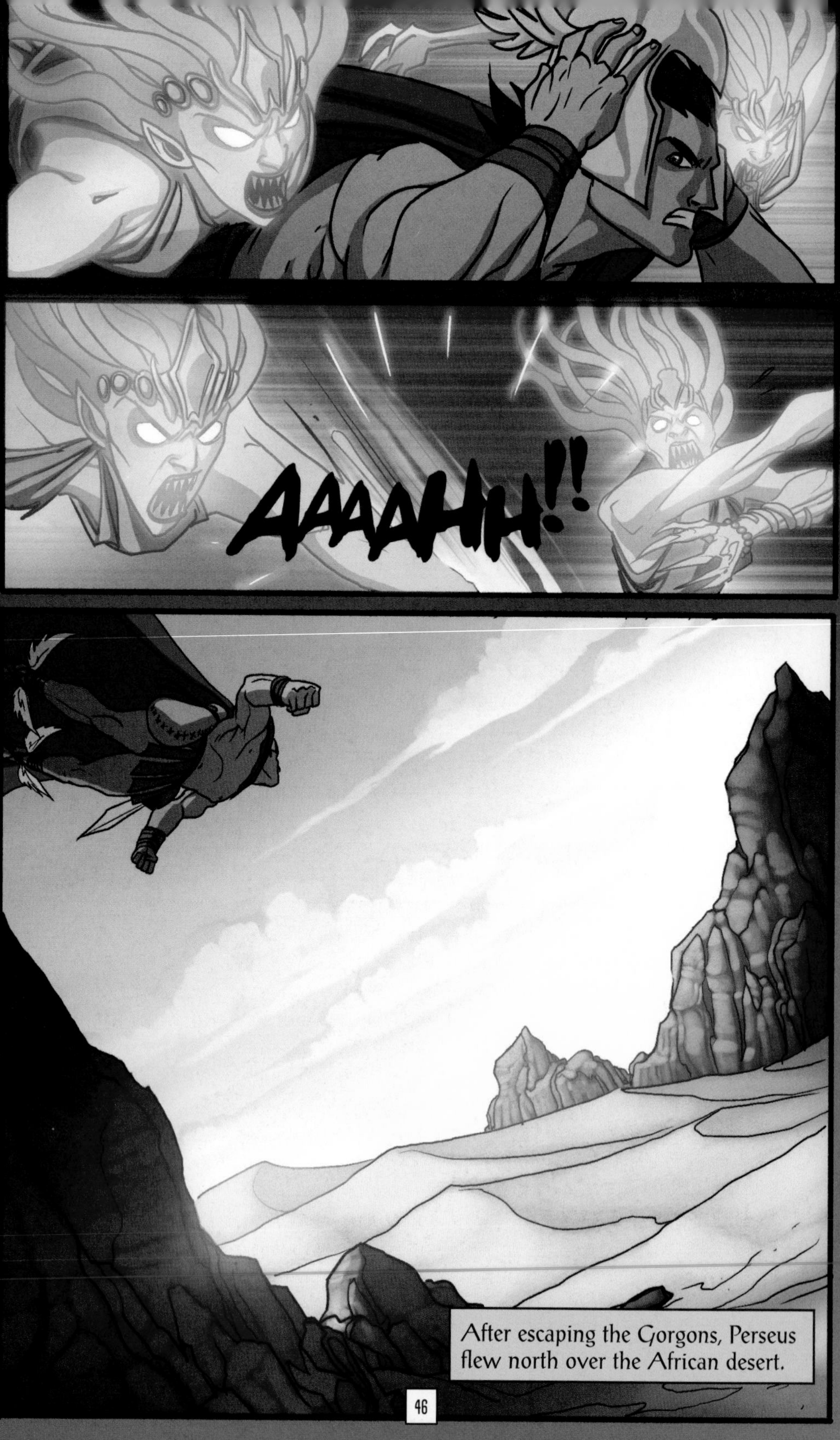
AAAAHH!!
After escaping the Gorgons, Perseus flew north over the African desert.

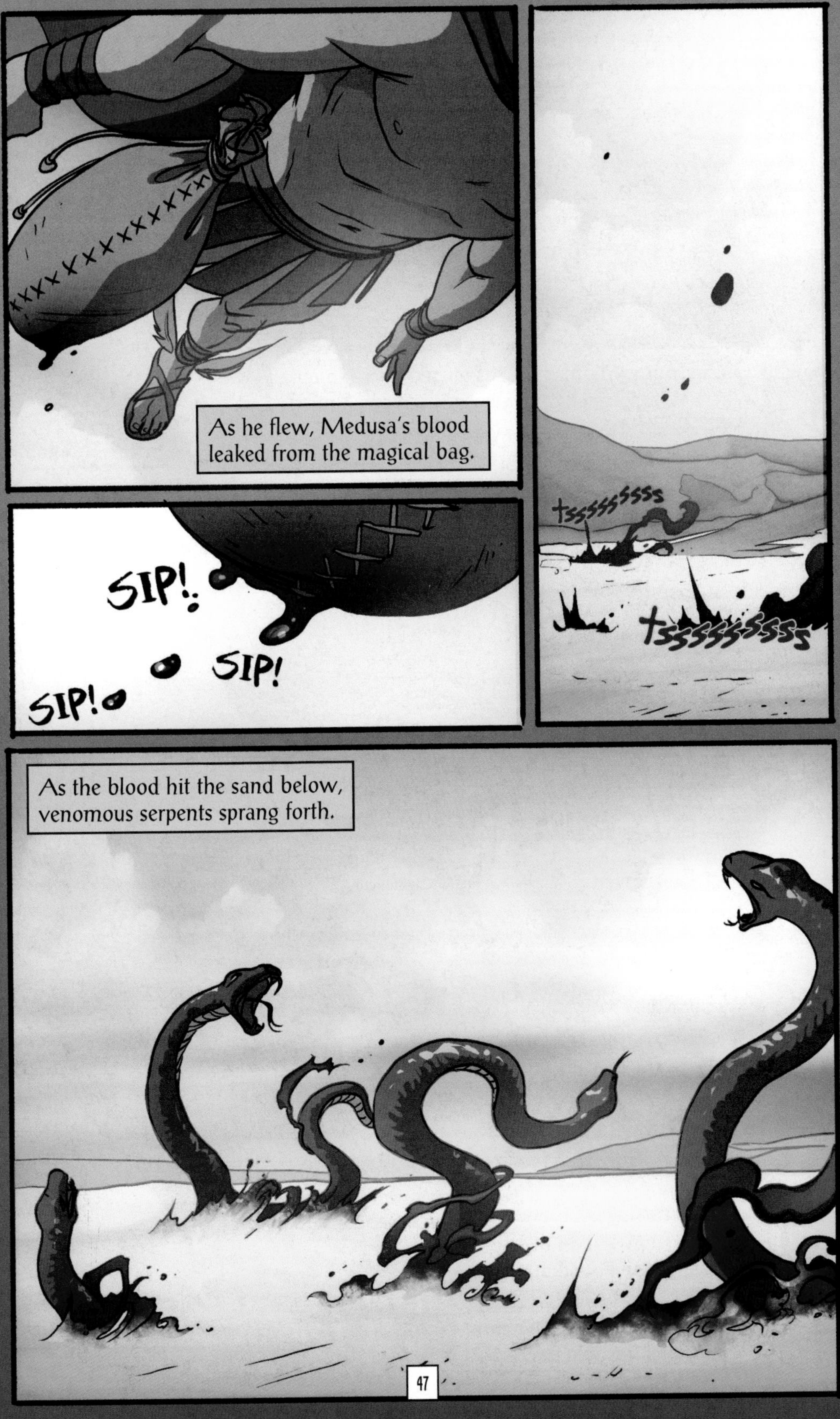

As he flew, Medusa's blood leaked from the magical bag.
SIP!
SIP!
SIP!
tssssssssss
tsssssssssss
As the blood hit the sand below, venomous serpents sprang forth.

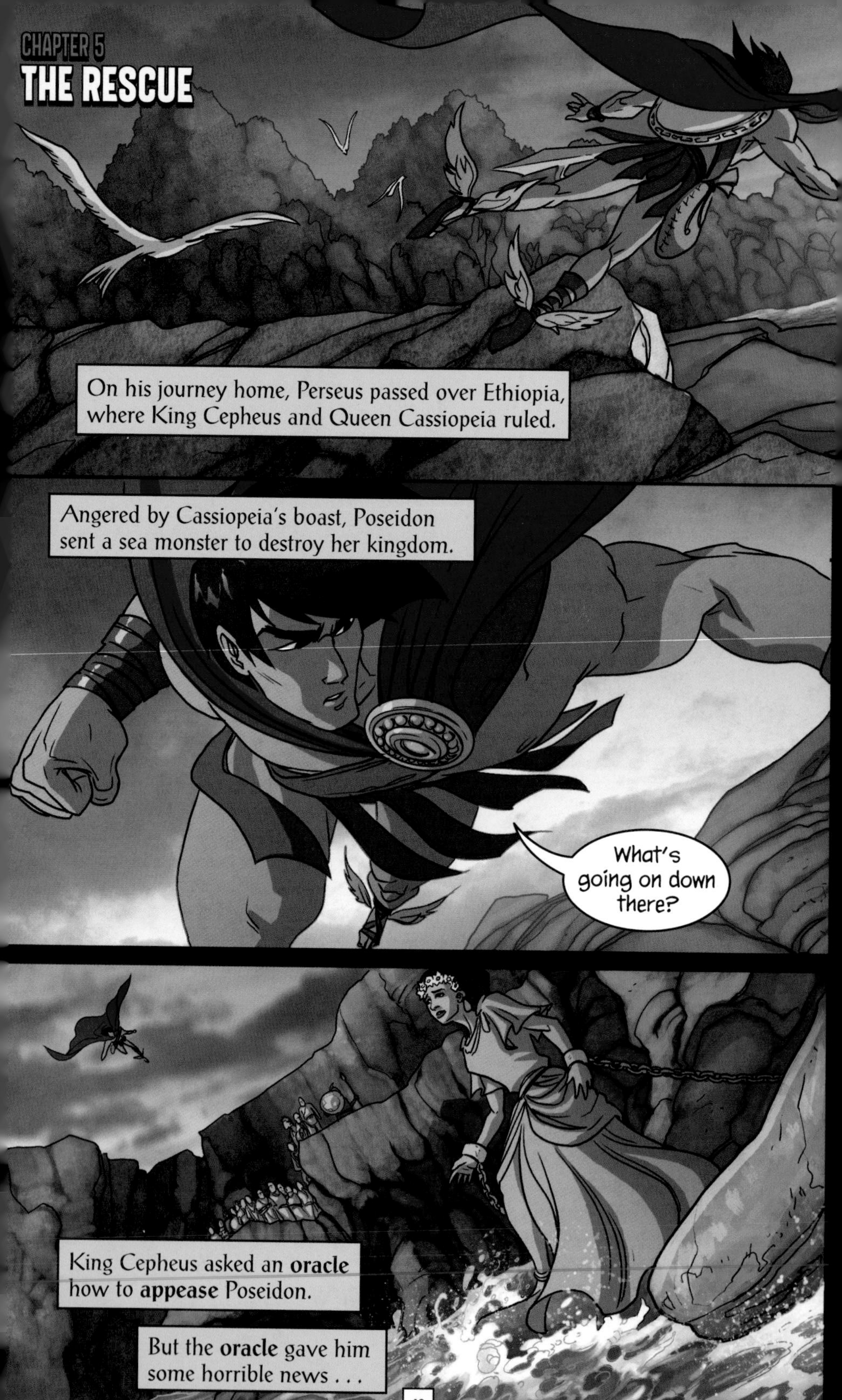
CHAPTER 5
THE RESCUE
On his journey home, Perseus passed over Ethiopia, where King Cepheus and Queen Cassiopeia ruled.
Angered by Cassiopeia's boast, Poseidon sent a sea monster to destroy her kingdom.
What's going on down there?
King Cepheus asked an **oracle** how to **appease** Poseidon.
But the **oracle** gave him some horrible news . . .

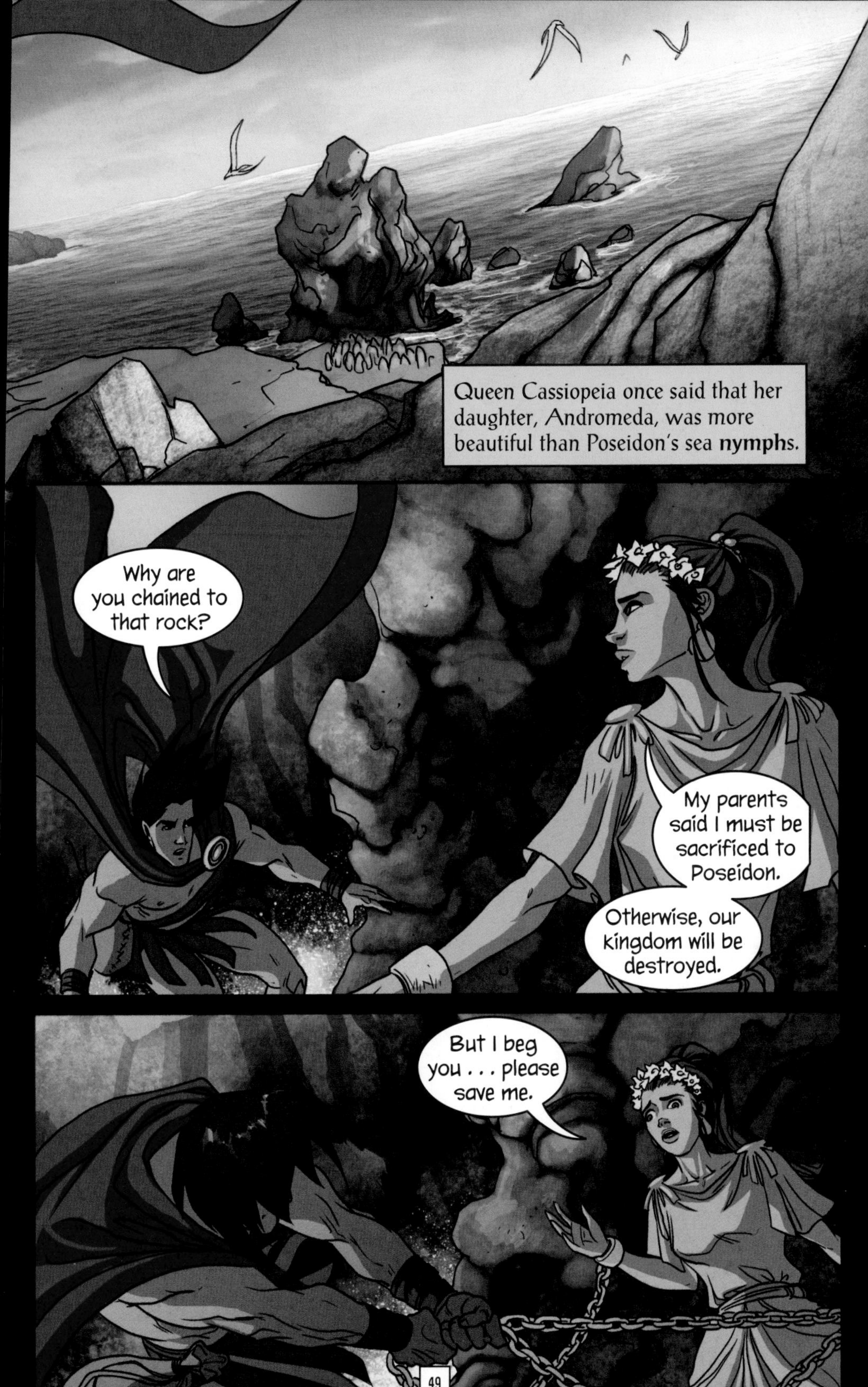
Queen Cassiopeia once said that her daughter, Andromeda, was more beautiful than Poseidon's sea **nymphs**.
Why are you chained to that rock?
My parents said I must be sacrificed to Poseidon.
Otherwise, our kingdom will be destroyed.
But I beg you . . . please save me.

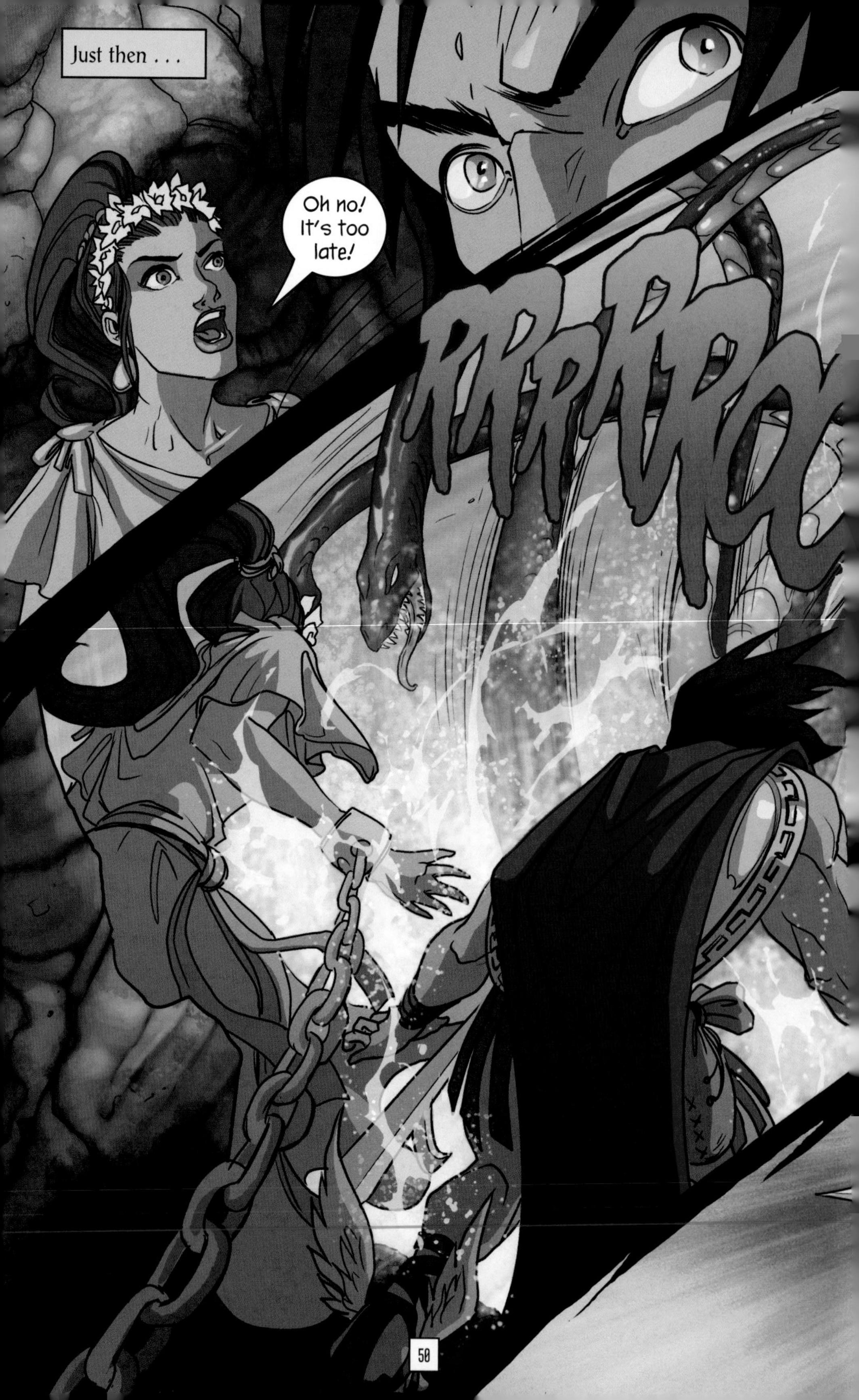
Just then . . .
Oh no! It's too late!

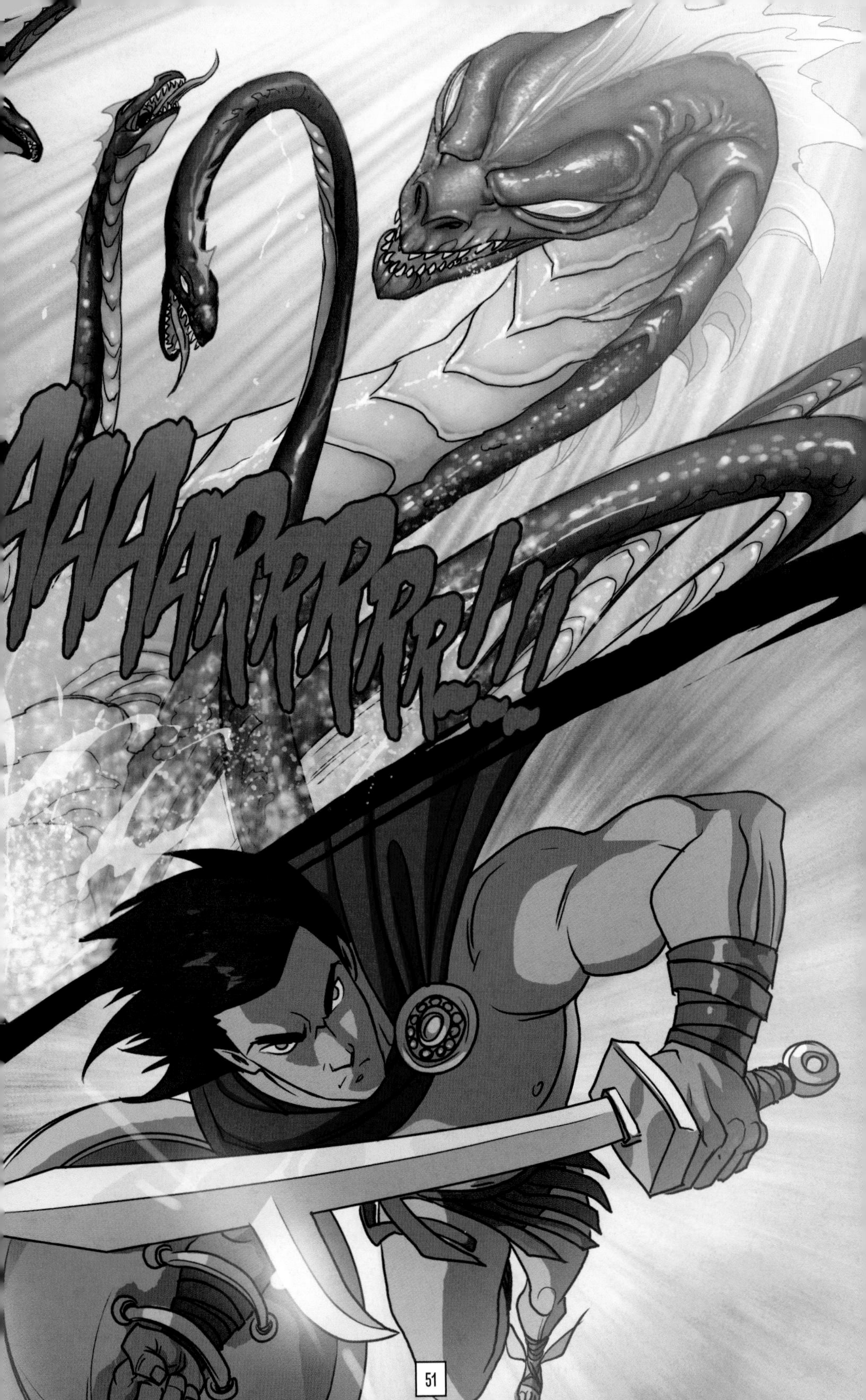
AAAARRRRR!!!

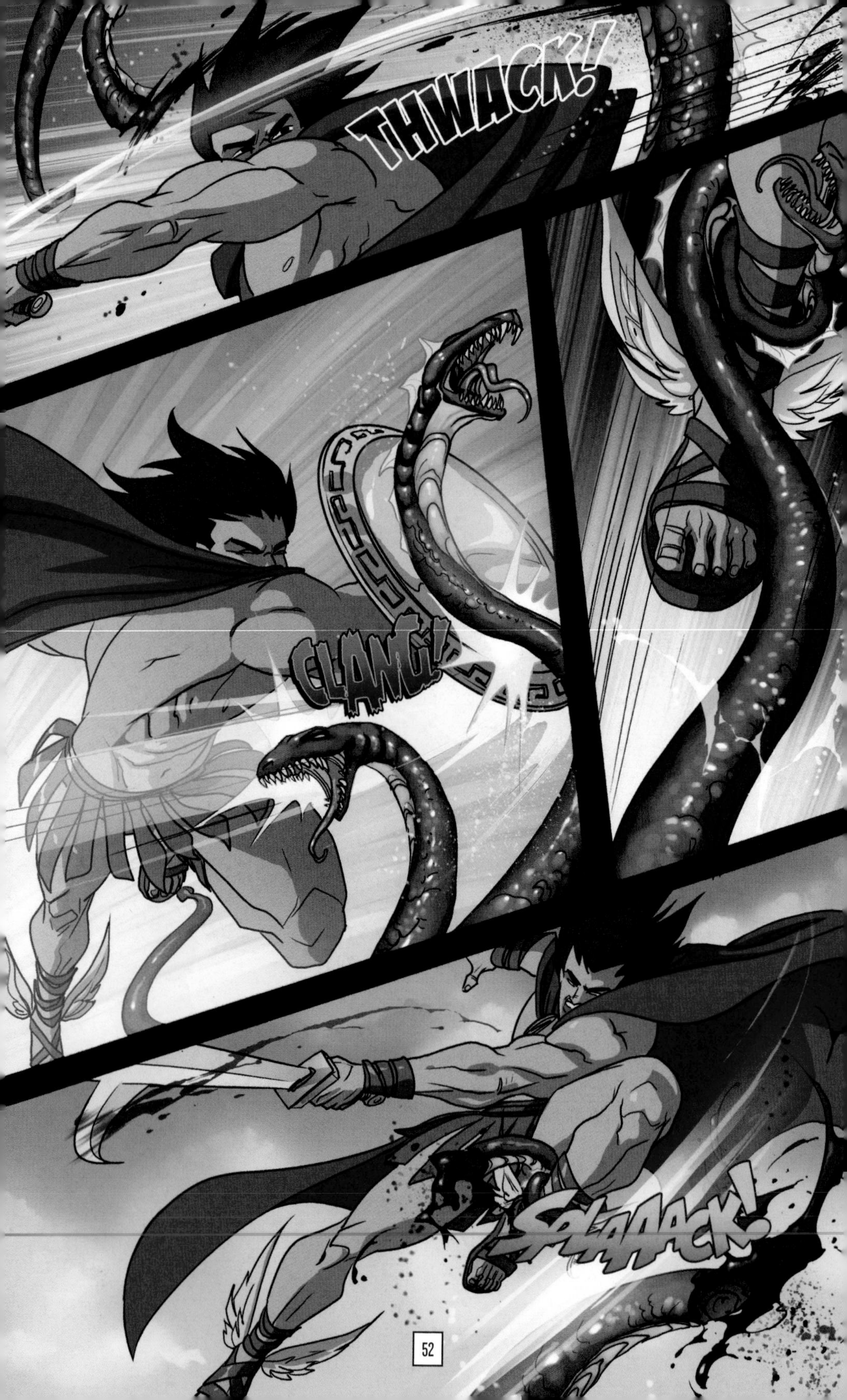
THWACK!
CLANG!
SPLAAACK!

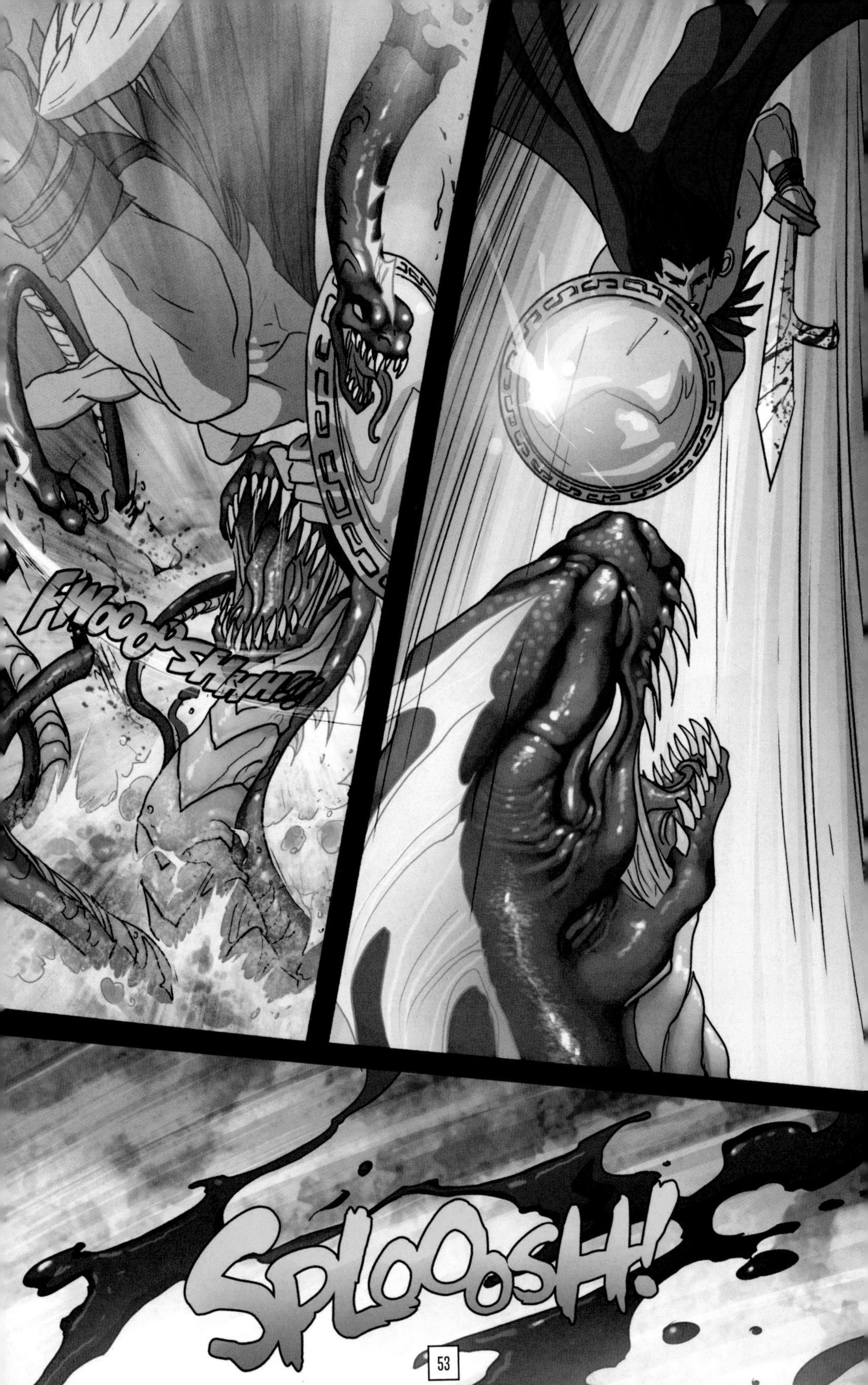
FWOOOSHHH!!
SPLOOOSH!

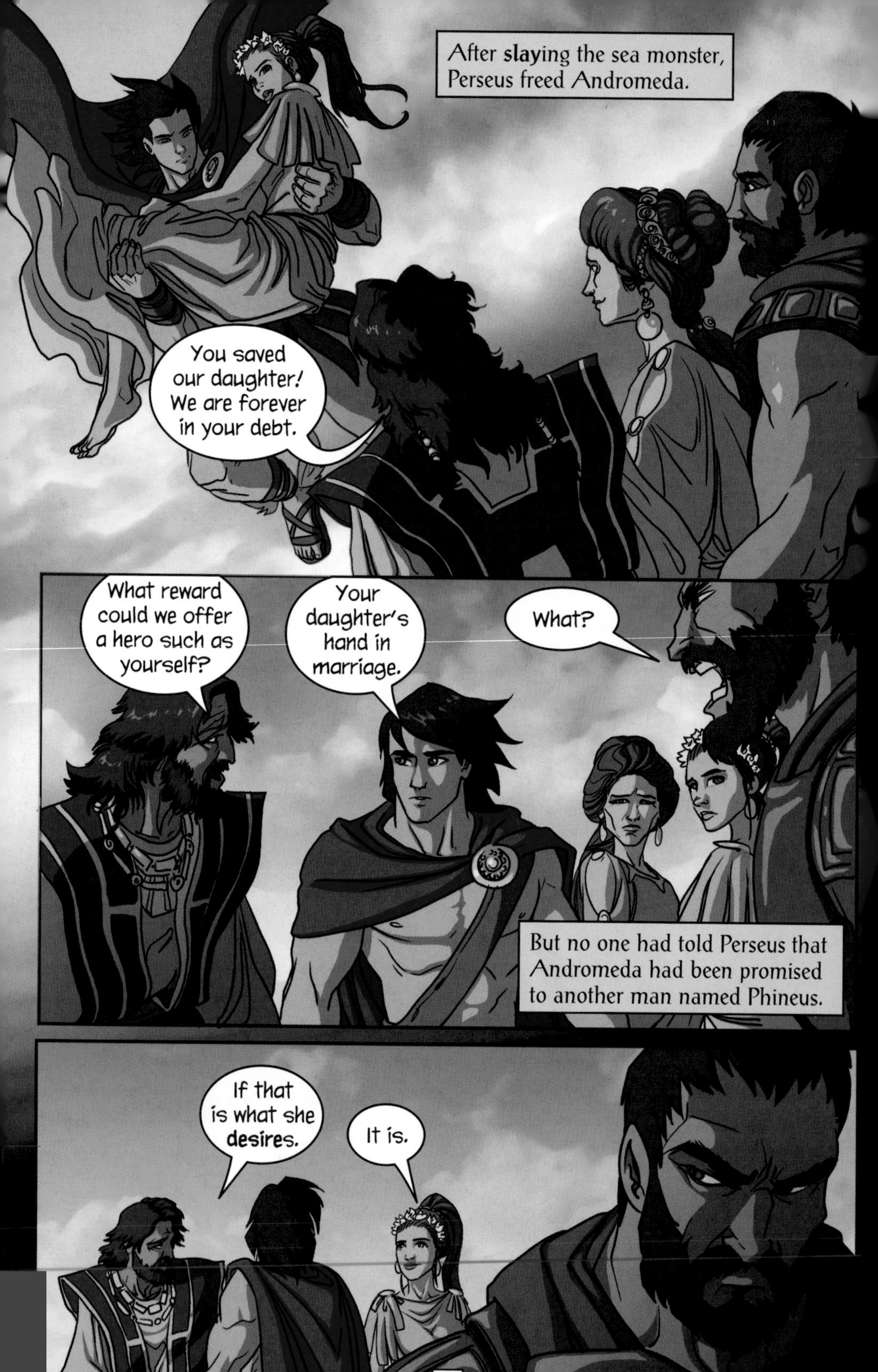
After **slay**ing the sea monster, Perseus freed Andromeda.
You saved our daughter! We are forever in your debt.
What reward could we offer a hero such as yourself?
Your daughter's hand in marriage.
What?
But no one had told Perseus that Andromeda had been promised to another man named Phineus.
If that is what she **desires**.
It is.

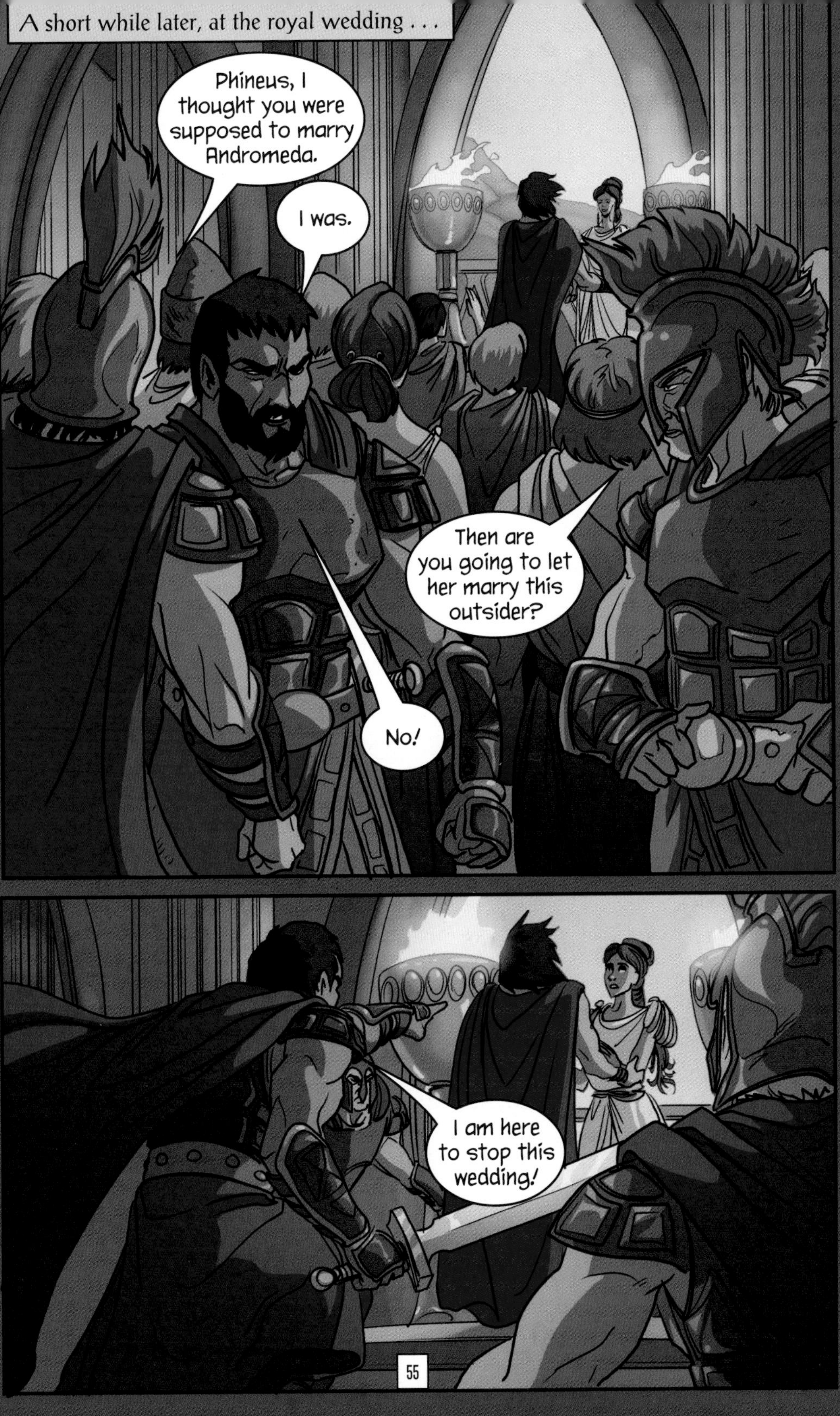
A short while later, at the royal wedding . . .
Phineus, I thought you were supposed to marry Andromeda.
I was.
Then are you going to let her marry this outsider?
No!
I am here to stop this wedding!

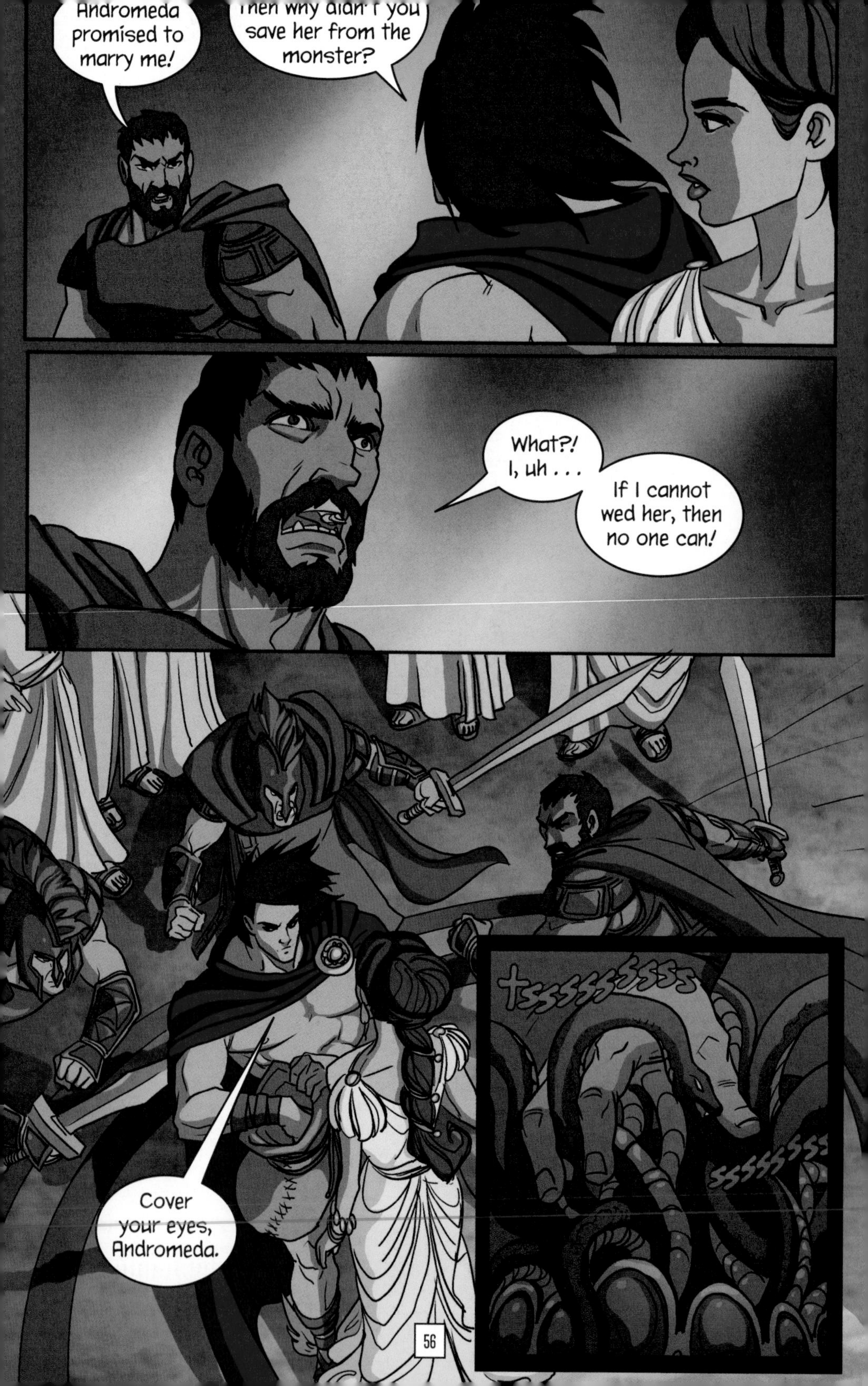
Andromeda promised to marry me!
Then why didn't you save her from the monster?
What?! I, uh . . .
If I cannot wed her, then no one can!
Cover your eyes, Andromeda.
TSSSSSSSSSS
SSSSSSSSS

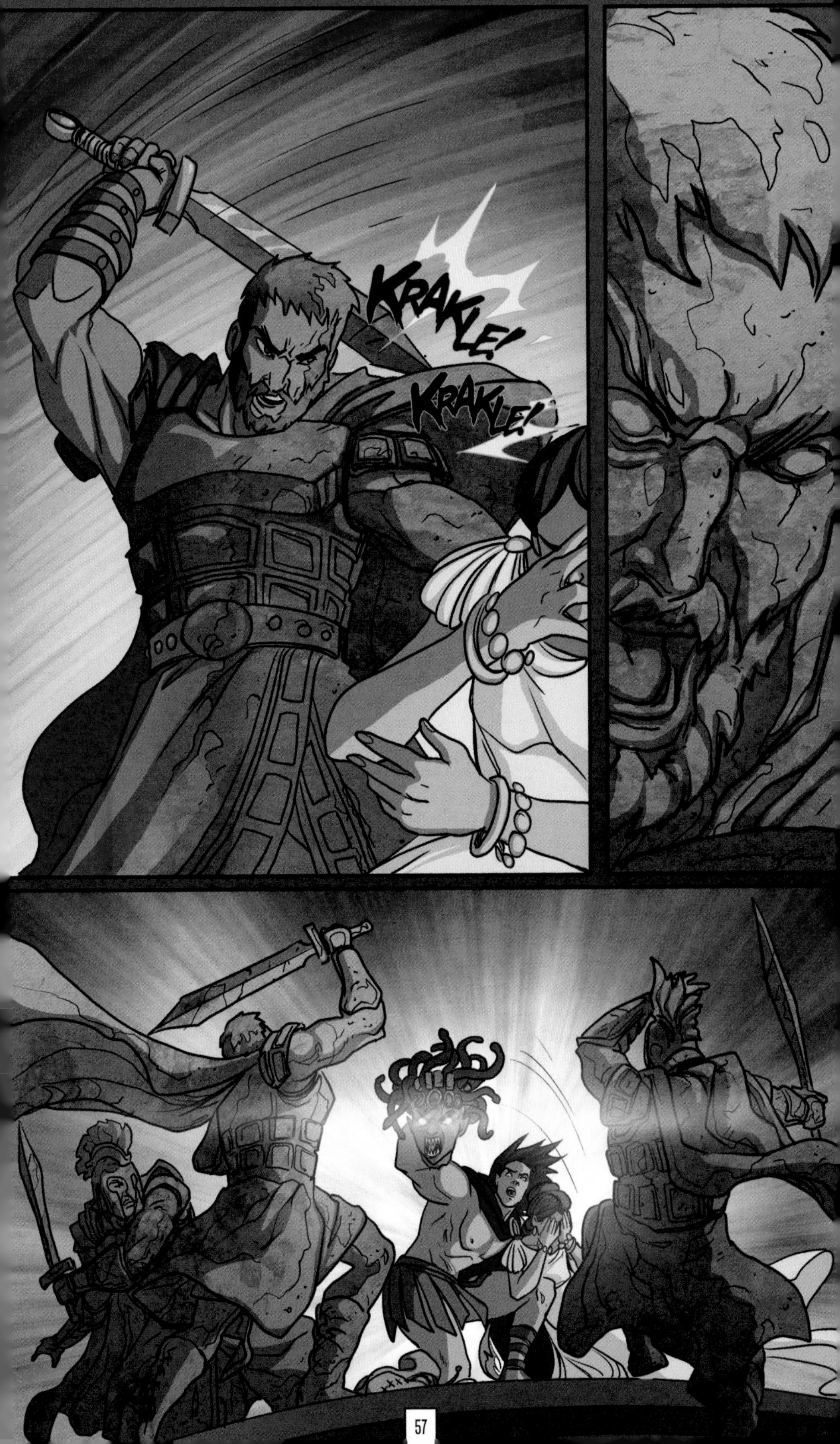
KRAKLE!
KRAKLE!

# CHAPTER 6
# THE EVIL KING

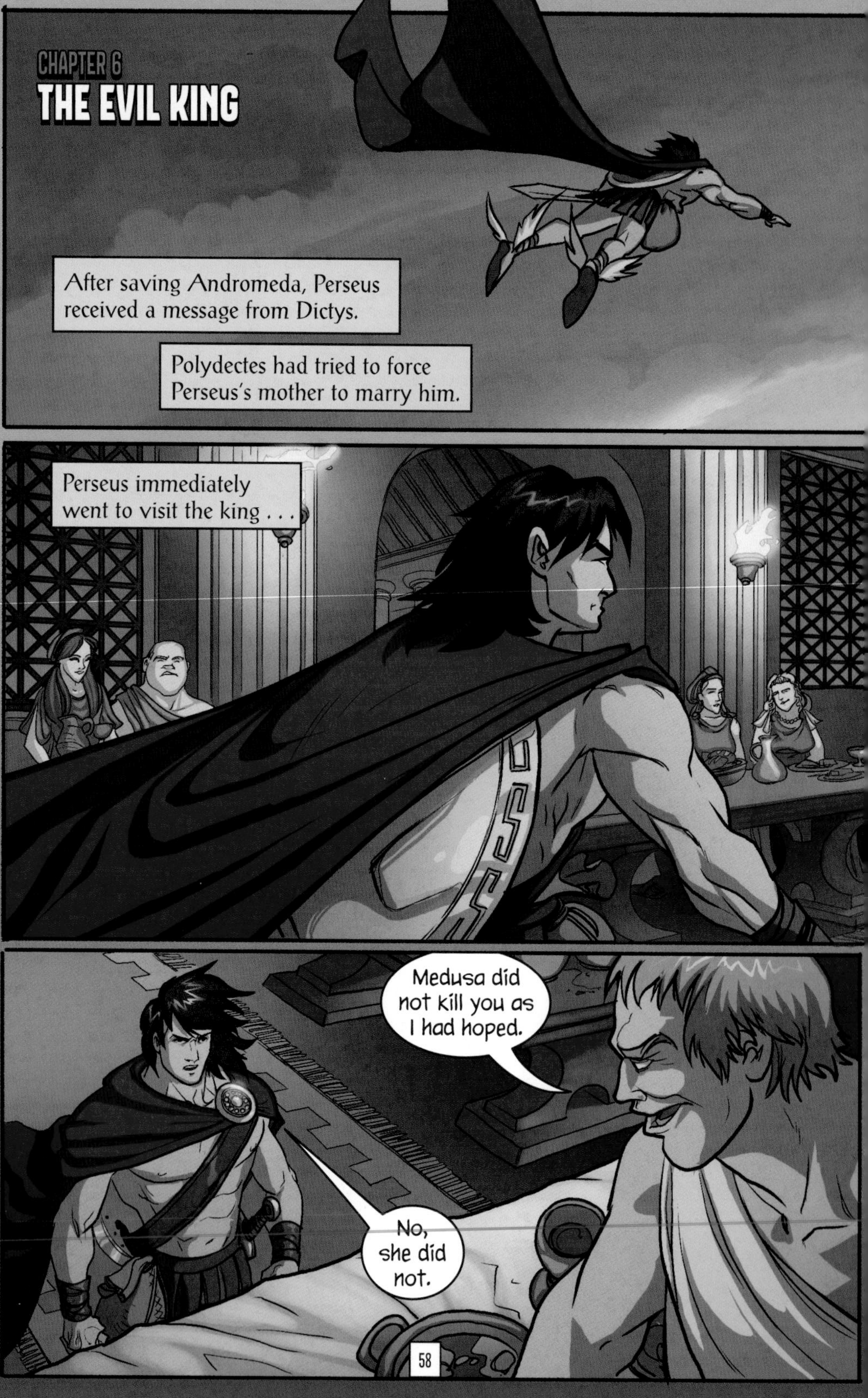
After saving Andromeda, Perseus received a message from Dictys.
Polydectes had tried to force Perseus's mother to marry him.
Perseus immediately went to visit the king . . .
Medusa did not kill you as I had hoped.
No, she did not.

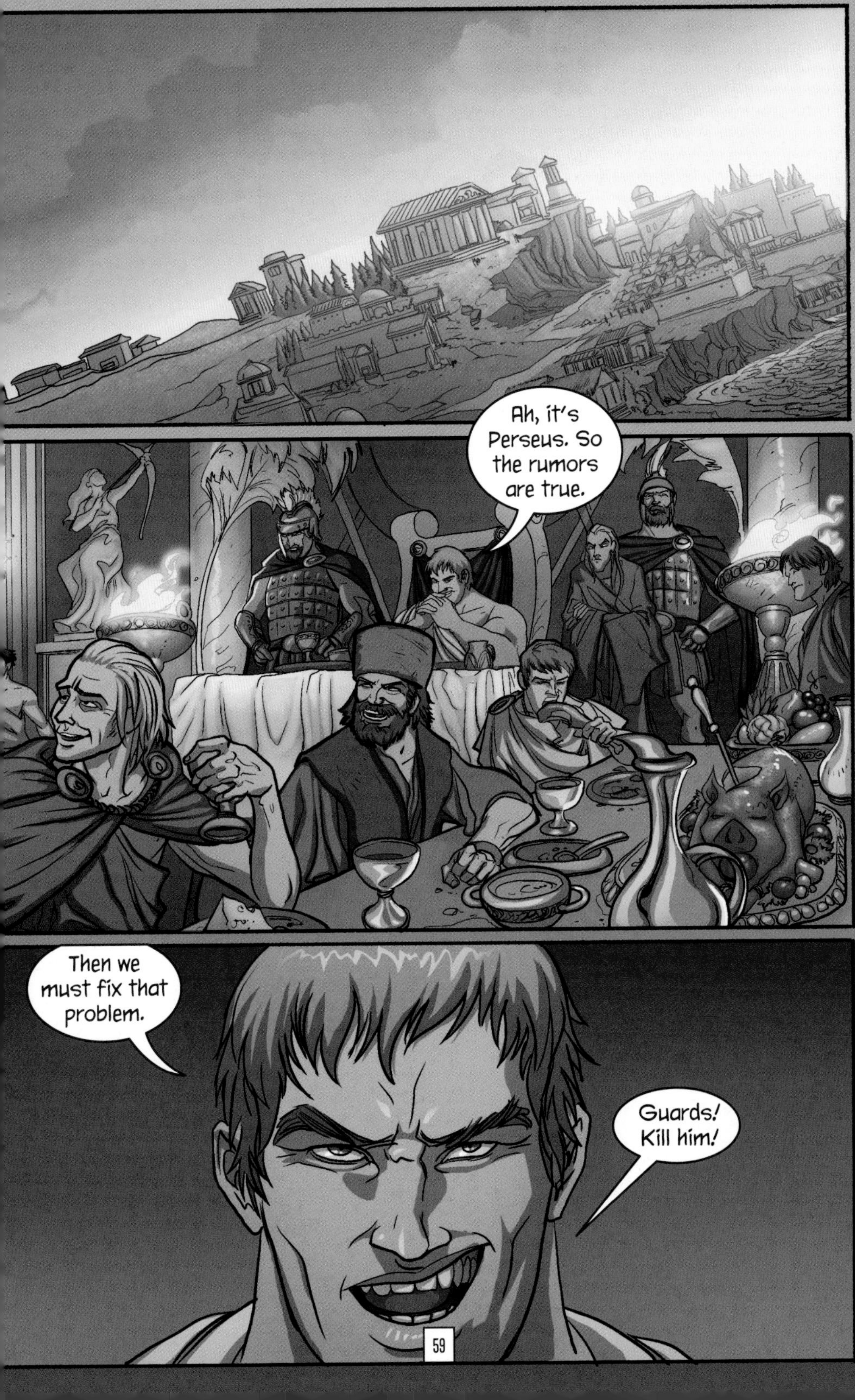
Ah, it's
Perseus. So
the rumors
are true.
Then we
must fix that
problem.
Guards!
Kill him!

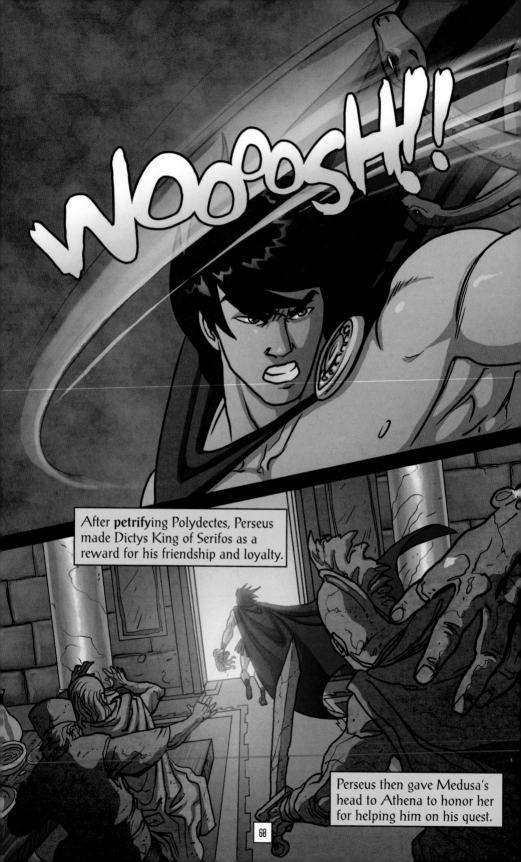

WOOOOSH!!

After **petrify**ing Polydectes, Perseus made Dictys King of Serifos as a reward for his friendship and loyalty.

Perseus then gave Medusa's head to Athena to honor her for helping him on his quest.

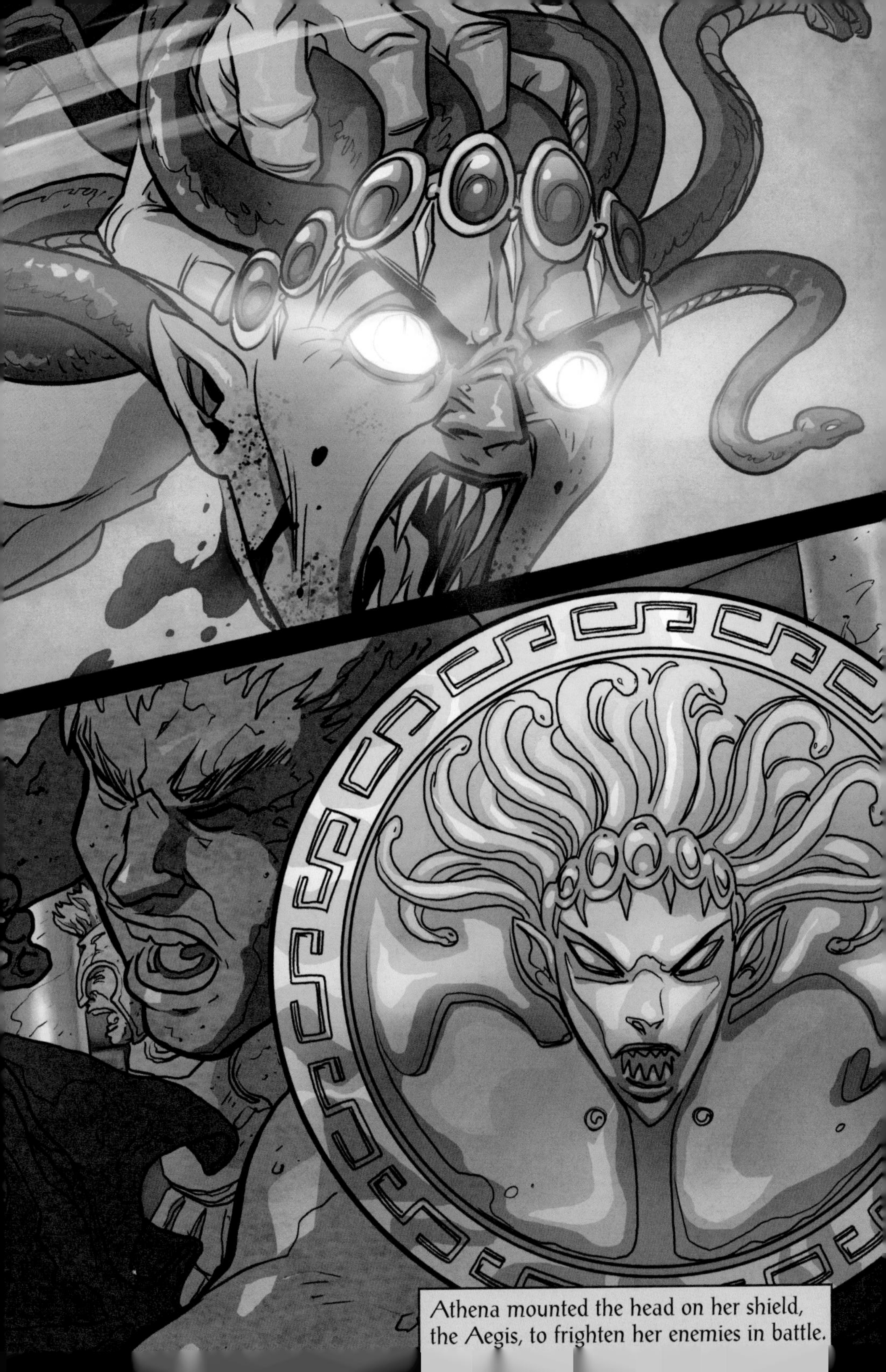
Athena mounted the head on her shield, the Aegis, to frighten her enemies in battle.

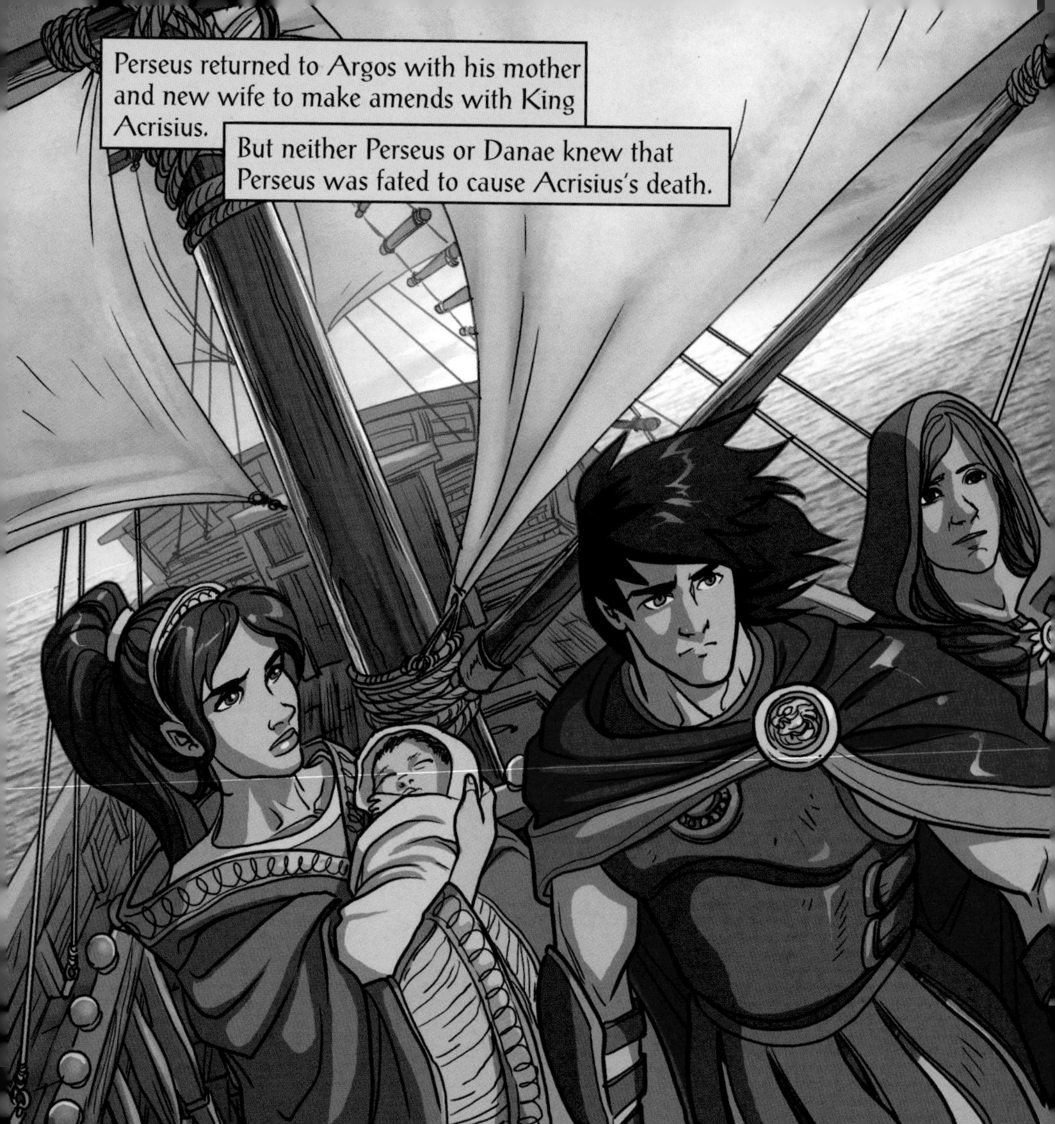
Perseus returned to Argos with his mother and new wife to make amends with King Acrisius.
But neither Perseus or Danae knew that Perseus was fated to cause Acrisius's death.

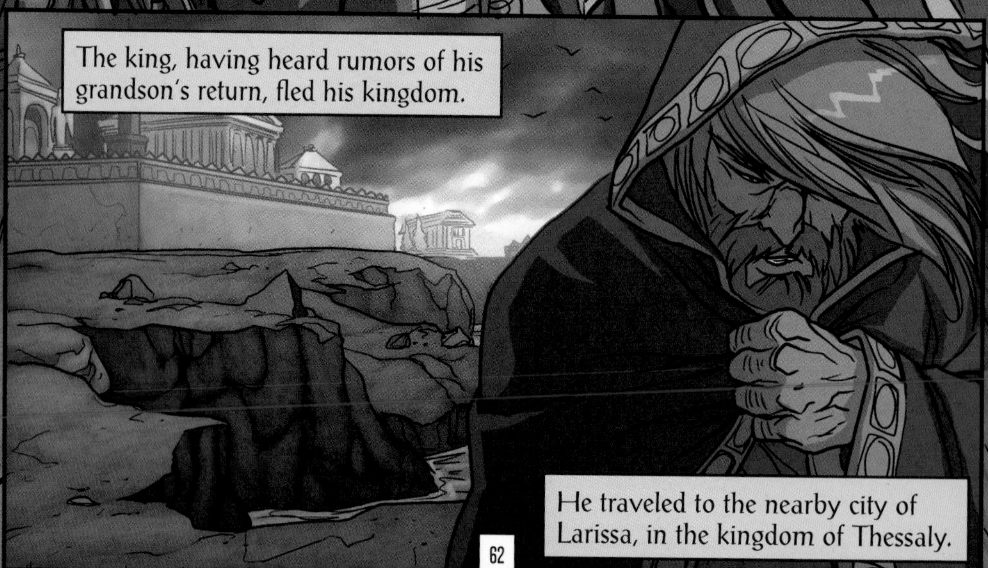
The king, having heard rumors of his grandson's return, fled his kingdom.
He traveled to the nearby city of Larissa, in the kingdom of Thessaly.

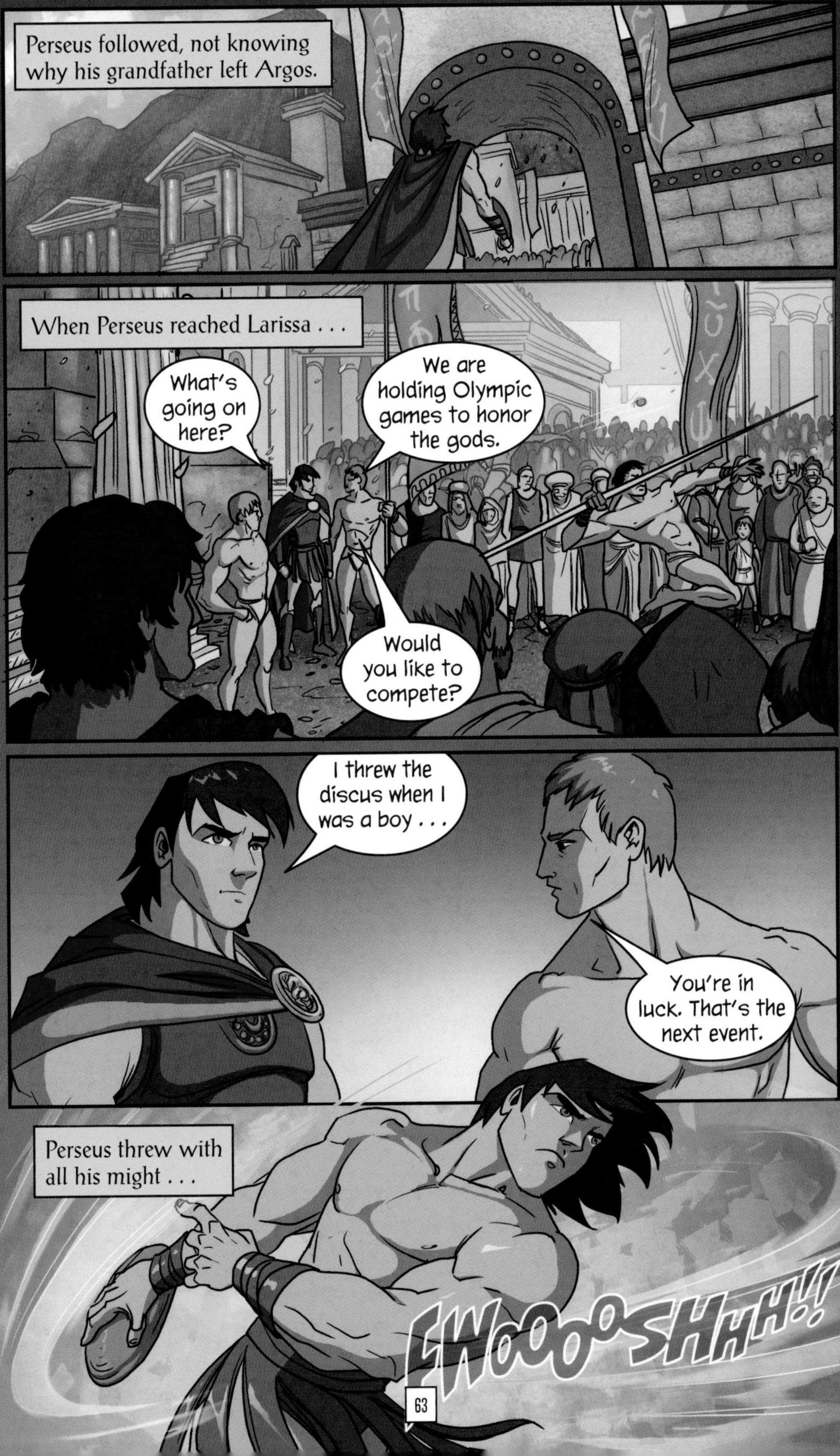

Perseus followed, not knowing why his grandfather left Argos.
When Perseus reached Larissa . . .
What's going on here?
We are holding Olympic games to honor the gods.
Would you like to compete?
I threw the discus when I was a boy . . .
You're in luck. That's the next event.
Perseus threw with all his might . . .
FWOOOOSHHH!!

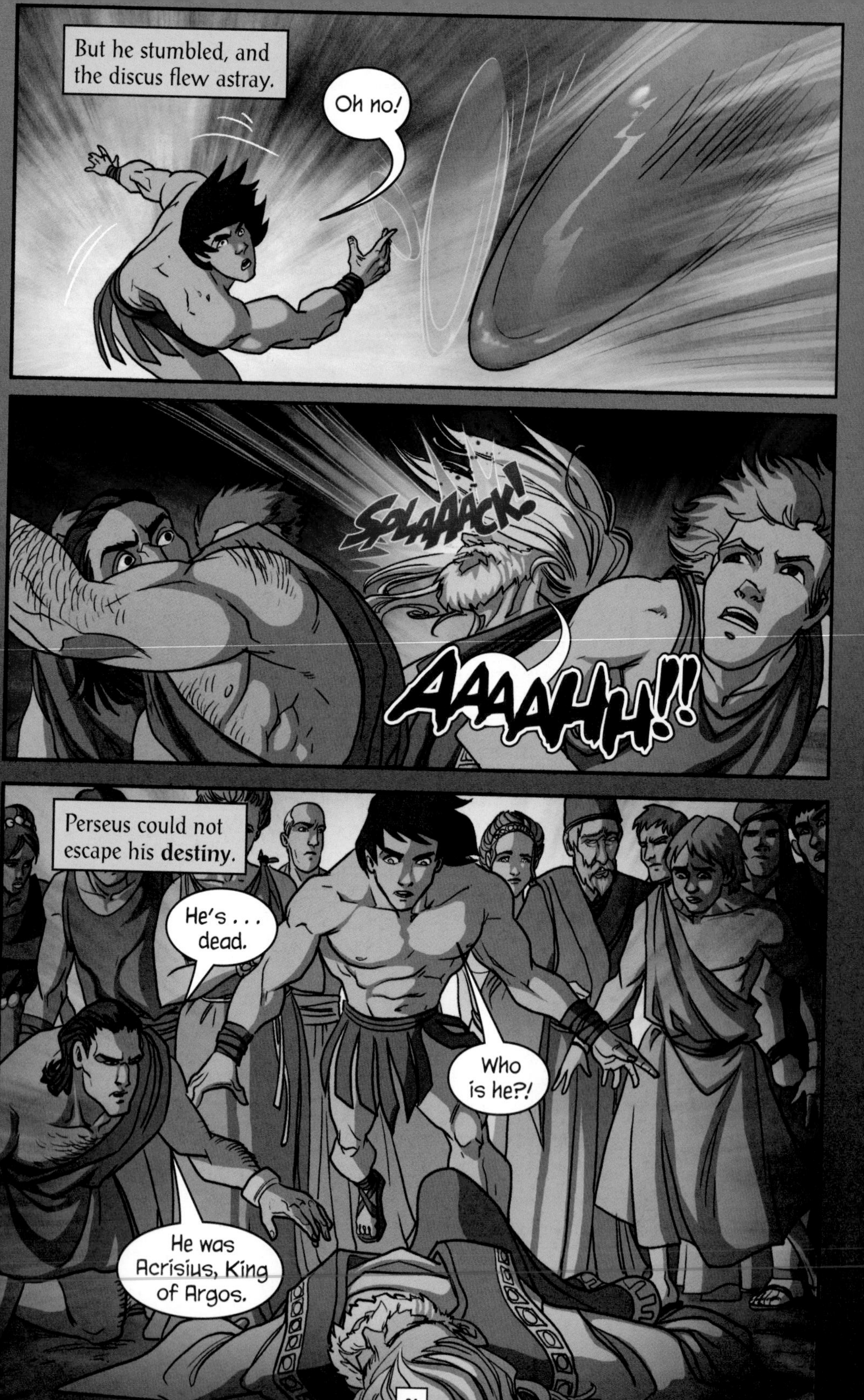
But he stumbled, and the discus flew astray.
Oh no!
SPLAAACK!
AAAAHH!!
Perseus could not escape his destiny.
He's . . . dead.
Who is he?!
He was Acrisius, King of Argos.

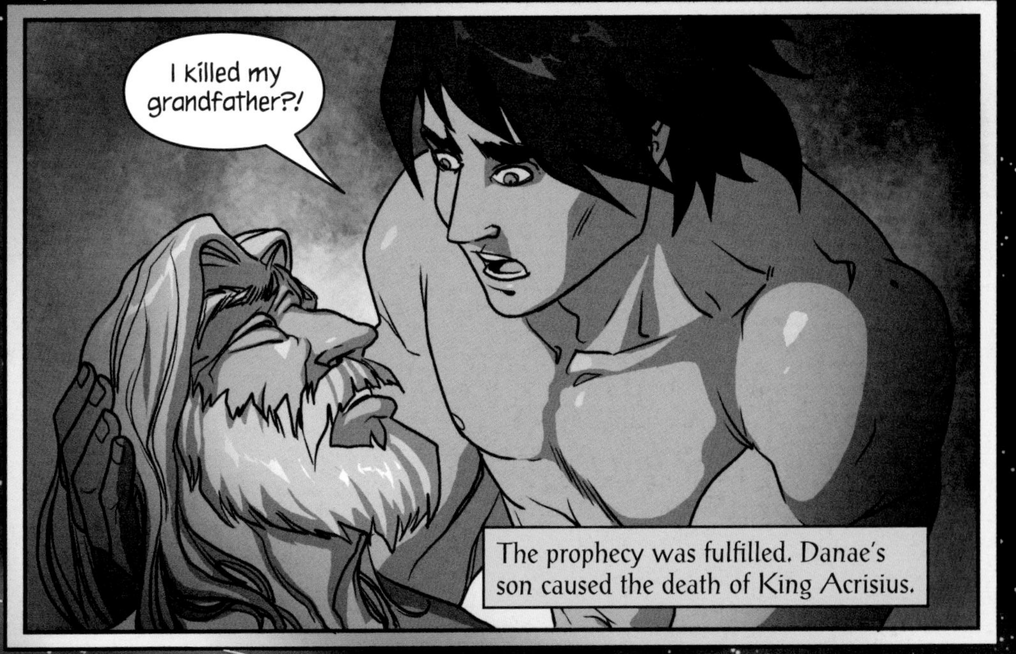
I killed my grandfather?!
The prophecy was fulfilled. Danae's son caused the death of King Acrisius.

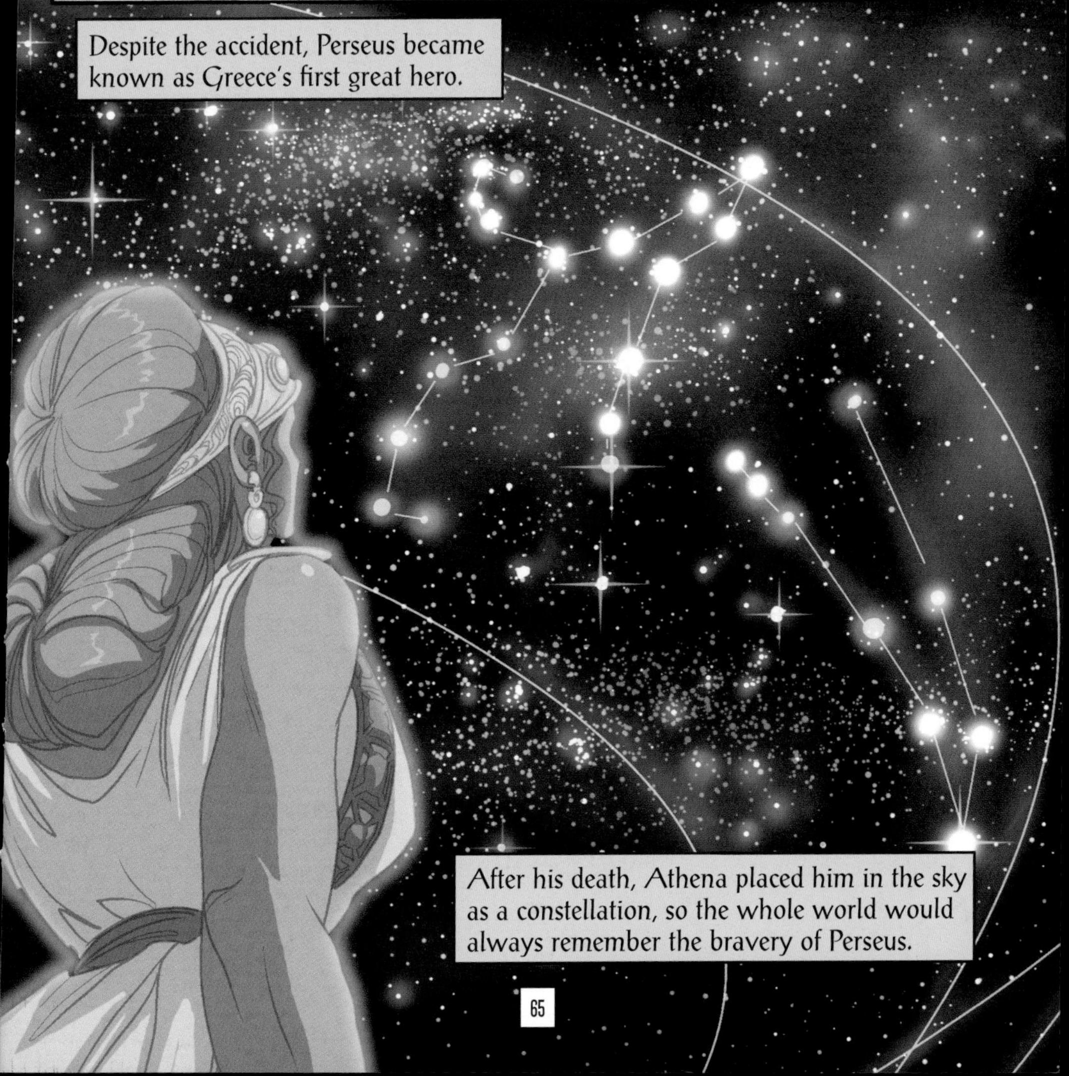
Despite the accident, Perseus became known as Greece's first great hero.
After his death, Athena placed him in the sky as a constellation, so the whole world would always remember the bravery of Perseus.

## ABOUT THE RETELLING AUTHOR AND ILLUSTRATOR

**Blake A. Hoena** grew up in central Wisconsin, where, in his youth, he wrote stories about trolls lumbering around in the woods behind his parent's house. Later, he moved to Minnesota to pursue a Masters of Fine Arts degree in Creative Writing from Minnesota State University, Mankato. Since graduating, Blake has written many books for children, including a retelling of "The Legend of Sleepy Hollow."

**Daniel Ferran** was born in Monterrey, Mexico, in 1977. For more than a decade, Ferran has worked as a colorist and an illustrator for comic book publishers such as Marvel, Image, Dark Horse, and Protobunker Studio.

# GLOSSARY

**appease** (uh-PEEZ)—satisfy or please someone

**desire** (di-ZIRE)—a strong wish or need for something

**destiny** (DESS-tuh-nee)—fate, or something that is guaranteed to happen

**domain** (doh-MAYN)—land or territory owned or guarded by someone

**hideous** (HID-ee-uhss)—ugly or horrible

**lair** (LAIR)—a place where something or someone eats and sleeps

**nymph** (NIMF)—a female spirit or goddess who is closely related to nature

**oracle** (AWR-uh-kuhl)—a person who learns the future by communicating with the gods

**petrify** (PET-ruh-fye)—turn to stone

**slay** (SLAY)—kill in a violent way

# COMMON CORE ALIGNED
# READING QUESTIONS

1. **Why does King Acrisius lock Danae in a tall bronze tower? Be sure to cite evidence from the art and text.** *("Refer to details and examples in a text when explaining what the text says explicitly and when drawing inferences from the text.")*

2. **Which character is more interesting to you: Perseus or Medusa? What character traits do they have that make you interested in them?** *("Describe in depth a character, setting, or event in a story.")*

3. **Human abilities and godlike abilities are two powerful main ideas in** *Perseus and Medusa.* **Can you find two examples in the graphic novel for each of these main ideas? List page numbers where you found your examples.** *("Determine a theme of a story.")*

4. **Who is Dictys? What does he do in the story? If you were asked to describe his personality, what would you say?** *"Describe in depth a character . . . drawing on specific details in the text."*

5. **Whose head does Perseus set out to slay? Why?** *("Refer to details and examples in a text when explaining what the text says explicitly and when drawing inferences from the text.")*

## COMMON CORE ALIGNED
# WRITING QUESTIONS

1. Should Perseus have set out to obtain Medusa's head? Why or why not? Write a short list of pros and cons, then explain your answer. *("Write opinion pieces on topics or texts, supporting a point of view with reasons and information.")*

2. Write an email to a family member to explain which Greek god in this story is the most powerful. What evidence or reasons does the story contain to support your choice? *("Produce clear and coherent writing in which the development and organization are appropriate to task, purpose, and audience.")*

3. Summarize the graphic novel *Perseus and Medusa* in a one-page essay. Make sure to write what happens in the story in the correct order of events. *("Write informative/explanatory texts to examine a topic and convey ideas.")*

4. You are invited to the wedding of Perseus and Andromeda. As a wedding guest, you have the unique opportunity to write a narrative (a detailed description of events) about what happens at the wedding. *("Write narratives to develop real or imagined experiences or events.")*

5. Write a letter to a friend explaining Perseus's heroics. Be sure to mention at least three adventurous acts. *("Produce clear and coherent writing in which the development and organization are appropriate to task, purpose, and audience.")*

# READ THEM ALL!

JULES VERNE'S
20,000 LEAGUES UNDER THE SEA
A GRAPHIC NOVEL
MARK TWAIN'S
THE ADVENTURES OF TOM SAWYER
A GRAPHIC NOVEL
ANNA SEWELL'S
BLACK BEAUTY
A GRAPHIC NOVEL
VICTOR HUGO'S
THE HUNCHBACK OF NOTRE DAME
A GRAPHIC NOVEL
ROBIN HOOD
A GRAPHIC NOVEL
ROBERT LOUIS STEVENSON'S
TREASURE ISLAND
A GRAPHIC NOVEL
MARY SHELLEY'S
FRANKENSTEIN
A GRAPHIC NOVEL
JULES VERNE'S
JOURNEY TO THE CENTER OF THE EARTH
A GRAPHIC NOVEL
ROBERT LOUIS STEVENSON'S
THE STRANGE CASE OF DR. JEKYLL AND MR. HYDE
A GRAPHIC NOVEL
BY BOWEN & FERRAN
WASHINGTON IRVING'S
THE LEGEND OF SLEEPY HOLLOW
A GRAPHIC NOVEL
DRACULA
JONATHAN SWIFT'S
GULLIVER'S TRAVELS
A GRAPHIC NOVEL
ARTHUR CONAN DOYLE'S
THE HOUND OF THE BASKERVILLES
A GRAPHIC NOVEL

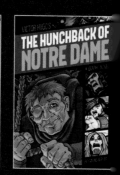

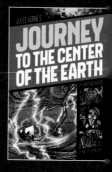

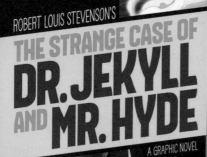

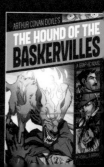